Harrier's Healer

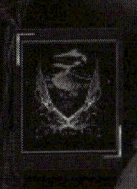

ALIYAH BURKE

Harrier's Healer

Aliyah Burke

Harrier's Healer

Copyright © 2009 by Aliyah Burke

All rights reserved. No part of this book may be reproduced or transmitted in any form or by any means without written permission of the author.

This book is a work of fiction. All characters, places and events are from the author's imagination and should not be confused with fact. Any resemblance to persons, living or dead, events or places is coincidental. All trademarks, service marks, registered trademarks, and registered service marks are the property of their respective owners and are used herein for identification purposes only.

Editor and Formatter: Savannah Frierson

Cover Artist: MMJ Designs

ISBN: 978-0-557-04199-2

To Valan,
For all the lives you touched while on earth.
Your love is eternal.
I miss you.

Acknowledgments

Any and all mistakes in this story are mine and not to be blamed on the ones who do this for a living. To my editor, for all the understanding and support you've shown me. Thank you! To my cover artist. Thank you!

Chapter One

Somewhere in the western Pacific...

"HMC Rogets, report to the bridge! HMC Rogets, report to the bridge!"

Shit, I just got off a ten-hour shift! What now? Alexis Rogets turned toward the loud squawk coming over the speaker as the baseball cap hid the narrowing of her eyes. Her shoulders rose and fell with the realization she had no choice; it wasn't her imagination or a voice in her head she was hearing.

"See you later," Alexis promised the group of people she stood amongst. They nodded and waved as she left to navigate the narrow stairwells and passageways. She paused at the entrance of the bridge, shaking her head over the noisy bustle that occurred.

"HMC Rogets reporting as ordered, sir." Commander Touchette, the captain of the USS *Everett* DDG, the destroyer she was assigned to, waved her forward as he read over the missive in front of him. He looked up when she stopped before him. Alexis waited patiently for him to speak.

"Chief Rogets," he greeted.

"Sir," she replied, waiting.

"I hate to do this to you considering you just got done in medical for the day, but the *Endeavor* has sent out a request for another doc. Since you know some of the men they are bringing in a little already, they want you." His blue eyes never left hers.

The USS *Endeavor* was an aircraft carrier. She'd served on one when she had been stationed out of Norfolk, Virginia, but had opted for a "small boy" this time—less people, a few hundred instead of a few thousand. Alexis believed she fit in well; however, being a doctor in the Navy didn't always give one the option of choosing where one served. They were sent where needed.

"When do I go, sir?"

"Now."

Now. Alexis maintained her emotionless facade. Her stuff was stowed away, so it would take very little for someone to send it to her. She was upset and a bit disappointed for she preferred being on the smaller vessel. "Very well, sir."

He regarded her closely. Alexis suspected he was watching for a flicker of surprise or anything suggesting shock,. He would once again be disappointed. She worked hard to make it seem nothing riled her, which was part of why the crew loved her. Alexis was level-headed and polite and even had a hint of a prankster when she felt she knew you well enough.

"Does anything surprise you, Rogets?" her CO asked with a grin.

"It's not good for me to get surprised," came her twinkling response. "Especially in my line of work."

Touchette shook his head in amusement. "I have yet to see anything faze you. Stay over there until things have calmed down a bit, and then give us a yell. We'll send a helo over for you." He smiled. "Don't want them thinking they're going to be allowed to keep the best doc in the Navy!" Alexis blushed and Touchette nodded. "Now, go on. Dismissed."

She did as commanded, shaking her head at his rare, explicit compliment. Chief Petty Officer Alexis "Lex" Milele Rogets was unique and she knew it. Generally, any full-fledged doctor would be an officer, but not her. She was finishing her schooling while enlisted and managed to graduate from Harvard as a doctor and a non-commissioned officer. Many believed that was one reason she was easy to get along with on both sides—officers and enlisted personnel. She was almost like a liaison between the two if needed, an exception to the rule and one she was happy with being.

USS *Endeavor* CVN

Snapping out a salute to the petty officer who met her on the flight deck, Chief Petty Officer Alexis Rogets made her way swiftly down to sickbay. *Here not even five minutes and I miss the destroyer,* she mused. Pushing open the door to the ship's medical room she was not sure what to expect.

Corpsmen were running all around and the place seemed chaotic to the untrained eye, but to her it was business like usual. Searching for the nearest khaki uniform, Alexis approached him and reported in. "Glad to have you aboard, Chief. I hear nothing but good things about you. Heard about you when I was stationed out in Norfolk," the tall ensign said.

"What's going on here, sir?" She waved one dark hand to encompass the room. "Who are the injured?"

Before he could respond, the most sinful voice in God's creation reached her, easily cutting through the surrounding noise. "Chief Rogets, glad to know you will be taking care of me." There was a slight hesitation. "And my men."

Well, Commander Touchette would be pleased to know that there is something to faze me. She took a deep breath and turned to face the man to whom the voice belonged. Commander Scott Leighton. Well, Lieutenant Commander Harrington Prescott Broderick Leighton III, if she were to be specific. A name she only knew from having seen his records.

Yeah, right!

For a mere moment Alexis was speechless. In front of her stood her very own secret erotic dream. All her fantasies about men ended up with her and this man in some amazing sexual act.

All six-foot-five inches of tanned body stood there covered with rippling muscles. Eyes that were cornflower blue and belonged in the bedroom only topped off his god-like body. Everything about his physique and presence screamed virile, sensual, and downright mouthwatering. *All he would have to do is crook his finger and I would follow him anywhere.*

Not even the black paint streaked on his face or his filthy blond hair could take away from his magnetic pull on her. And it had been like that since the day they met. *Can't think about that now, Lex; need to acknowledge him before he gets suspicious,* she admonished herself with a mental shake to bring her back to business at hand.

"Commander Leighton," she said. "I will go see what I can do to help your men." She cast a questioning glance at the ensign, who pointed her to the area she'd be using. She hurried off without responding to either officer, knowing she could get away with it because of the rush to attend to the injured men.

Pushing back the curtain, she reached for a pair of medium surgical gloves. Alexis turned back to get her first patient and froze. Commander Leighton stood before her. "What do you need, Commander? I am just about to go grab one of your men."

A sexy half smile crossed his face. "I'm the only one from my team left who needs attention. The rest of the men here are the ones we rescued. So I'm all yours…" Again that almost indiscernible hesitation. "…Chief."

If that were only so. "Sit down." She was all business. "What happened?"

"I got a few scrapes, nothing too serious." His blue eyes burned a hole into her as he spoke.

"Uh-huh," she muttered, moving towards him. What was "nothing serious" in the SEAL way of thinking was *much* different than what it might mean to her as a doctor.

Lieutenant Commander Scott "Harrier" Leighton felt the familiar butterflies reemerge in his belly. Strangely enough, the fluttering only happened when this woman was around. He didn't understand it, he towered over her by almost a foot and outweighed her by almost one hundred pounds, yet here he sat, nervous as a child on their first day of school.

His blue eyes roved over her as she approached. She wore her dark hair secured tightly off her face and hidden way under a cap marked USS *Everett* DDG. He preferred her hair down, though; it was thick and fell gently around her face and shoulders. Or it had the last time he'd seen it free. She looked so feminine that way — not that she didn't now, for she was hot in anything — but she looked gentle with her hair unbound.

Her face was, to him, perfect. Thick eyelashes framed her exotic tiger-eyed gaze. Scott reflected on that cute nose and those succulent full lips he'd wanted to kiss the very first time he'd seen her. This was the eighth time they'd met, and that desire was just as strong today as it had been the first day. Scott knew it was only a matter of time before he gave into that yearning.

She was five-seven and had all the right curves in all the right places. Her breasts were full and her hips made him imagine nothing except his hands holding them as he drove into her body as deeply as he could go. Over and over, all night long. Her ass made his mouth go dry; it was flawless.

She *was* the total package. Beautiful, smart, energetic, strong, and very sexy. Topping it off, her body looked as if it had been covered with rich toffee. *I would sell my soul for one night with this ebony goddess.*

Scott knew all about her because he'd pulled up her file and read up on her. Upon graduation, she'd become a non-commissioned officer. In Scott's mind, this was why commissioned and non-commissioned officers respected her so much. She was the perfect liaison between the levels. He also knew when and where she was born, where she considered her permanent address to be, and how many family members she had. But all of that wasn't enough. Everything he'd learned was technical; he wanted to *know* this woman.

He blinked as he realized she was staring at him, waiting for a response. "I'm sorry, what?" *I sound like a moron!* he thought ruefully.

"I said you need to take off your shirt. There is a deep tear and I want to evaluate whether or not you require stitches," she informed him in a crisp and professional voice.

His eyes blazed with a heat that could have burned a hole right into the hull of the ship. "Sure, just a sec." He began to remove his shirt and couldn't stop the hiss of pain that slipped out from between his teeth.

Her fingers were there, brushing his out of the way as she searched. "Hang on, let me look." A couple of noncommittal murmurs left her mouth and went straight into his ears, traveling quickly to his groin. "This needs stitches." She turned her head and their faces were inches apart.

The busy room seemed to fade away into silence as their twin gazes bore into each other. It would take nothing to lean in and taste her lips, but Alexis pulled her head back abruptly. "Take it off," she ordered in a brisk tone.

One eyebrow, covered with paint, arched as he said, "What?"

"Your shirt. Take it off and I will clean the wound and get someone to stitch you up," she elaborated insistently.

Oh, hell no! I am not about to let you weasel your way out of looking at or touching my body! "I want you..." That damn hesitation again, "To do it."

"Why me? There are plenty of corpsmen who can stitch a wound just fine. There are other people in here hurt worse than you."

"I remember how well you took care of Cade on the carrier in the Caribbean."

He and his men had just rescued his second-in-command and best friend Tyson Kincade, along with his wife Jayde, from the mountains of Belize. Her previous duty had been on that aircraft carrier; now she was here in a different ocean and still making him tremble. "Very well," she said reluctantly.

Scott quirked an eyebrow. "You're not scared of touching me are you, Alexis?" his deep tone purred.

Her eyes flew open wide at his use of her first name. It was as if her name was made to roll off his tongue. While there had always been an attraction between them, he'd never before done anything like this. It was such a breach of protocol. He would be in so much trouble if she were to report it. "Why would I be scared? Did you pick something up that I might catch?" she sassed him back as she helped him remove his shirt.

I can't believe those words came out of my mouth. At least she is joking about it. "I have never picked anything up. Ever." He was clear of any and all sexually transmitted diseases.

"I'm sure your wife or girlfriend is very pleased to know that," Alexis ventured primly.

He grimaced slightly as she applied the sterilizer to the gash. "You know I don't have a wife."

She didn't even look at him. "I don't know anything about you, Commander," she said, reminding them of the protocol.

His words were soft. "Don't lie to me or yourself."

"Don't move. And keep your arm where it is," she said as she threaded a needle. "Are you sure you don't want a local?"

"I'm sure. Just keep talking to me and I will be fine." *You could amputate my left leg if you talked to me through it. I just want to hear your seductive voice.*

"You're the boss," she muttered.

I will be soon. "Tell me about yourself then, so I can get to know you," he ordered as she slid the needle into his flesh.

"What has you so interested in my life, Sc…Commander?" Her eyes narrowed with concentration as she made tiny, even stitches in his side.

He heard her slip and smiled as he looked at the top of her head. "The same thing that has you interested in mine," he whispered, falling silent as another person walked into the small area.

"Chief Rogets," the corpsmen said. "We need your help with one of the other men."

"Is it an emergency, Corpsman?" she asked, not taking her eyes off her work.

"No, ma'am, just as soon as you can." He looked at the barechested man who sat on the bed while the woman sewed up his side. "Sir, ma'am." Then he was gone.

Finishing swiftly, Alexis tied off the last suture and cut it. Pushing away on her wheeled stool, Alexis rolled to the sink, removed the gloves from her hands, and washed them as she talked to the man sitting behind her. "There you go, Commander. Take it easy and you should be fine in a couple of weeks." Alexis reached for the towel and found him holding it out to her.

"Thanks for taking such good care of me," he murmured. He started to reach out and caress her until a yell from across the room snatched their attention.

"Lex! He's crashing!"

With barely a glance at the handsome SEAL, Alexis "Lex" Rogets dashed away to lend her expertise.

Picking up his discarded and possibly ruined shirt along with his pack, Scott gazed across the room and watched in amazement as she worked diligently on the man. Even when blood sprayed up at her she seemed unfazed. She was a damn good doctor, sexy as hell, and someday soon, his. With one final look, he left medical to hit the showers and check on the rest of his men.

Alexis knew the moment he left. Somehow, the room just felt emptier. Her hands deep in the chest she'd just cracked open, she wondered what twist of fate would bring them together next. That thought was brief and fleeting because her mind returned to the task before her. And although she was tired, she knew it wouldn't be an issue as her mind was still sharp. Residency hours had been much worse than this.

About an hour later, peeling off the blood-covered gloves and tossing them in the trash receptacle, Alexis rolled her head around trying to loosen up her neck muscles. They were done. All the men were stabilized. Hands washed, she applied lotion trying to preemptively ease the dryness.

"Great job, Lex," a masculine voice said from behind her.

A smile formed as she answered, "Thanks, Tom. You too." She turned and walked with him towards the door. A few corpsmen were cleaning up bloody gauze and washing down tables, but the room was silent now. "It was good to work with you again. I didn't know you were out here." Tom had served with her before on a carrier in Norfolk.

He flashed a grin, his white teeth standing out vividly against his dark skin. "Wanna get some chow?"

"Thanks, but no thanks, Tom. I'd just pulled a ten-hour stint on the *Everett* before they sent me here. I need to unwind before they send me back." She patted him on the arm.

"We will have to do something in port together. Grab a meal or something."

Lex nodded. "Great, you know how to reach me. I'll see ya around. By the way," she tossed over her shoulder as she walked off, "congrats on being frocked." He sent her back another sparkling grin as she moved away from him.

Shutting the hatch behind her, Alexis sighed. *I'll just give it a few minutes before I call Touchette for the helo.* Her gaze took in the sun as it began its evening descent. She loved it out here. This was one of her favorite spots, the fantail. There weren't many places on an aircraft carrier where one could feel alone, but this was one of them.

"Too bad I won't be here to fully watch the sunset," she said to the rushing wind.

"Why not?" a sexy baritone voice asked from behind her.

She jumped, hand pressed to her chest, unwittingly drawing Scott's gaze there. "*Jesú*, you scared me!" As her dark eyes landed on the man who stood before her, Alexis fought for sanity. "Excuse me, sir. Hello, Commander."

Scott's striking eyes glanced around as if making sure they were alone out there. Finding the answer to be to his satisfaction, he settled those beautiful blue eyes back on her body, setting it to burn with a heat that rivaled the late-afternoon sun. "Come on, now, Alexis." His hard body moved closer to her. "How long are we going to do this?"

Dear God, this man's voice is potent. "Do what, Commander?"

He took a deep breath and leaned on the rail beside her, almost but not quite touching her. "Why aren't you going to be around for the sunset?"

"I'm going back to the *Everett*. I just came out here to relax for a bit." Her body turned around and leaned on the rail like he did. "How are you feeling?"

"Good, you did a wonderful job." He shifted closer to her. "How long are we going to keep this up?" Leighton questioned.

I bet you can keep it up for a long, long time. Alexis cleared her throat. "I don't know."

"Do you remember the day we first met?" he asked, his focus directly on her.

"Yes. It was in Norfolk," she said, shifting a bit.

"I almost ran you over and you...well...you wanted to say something a lot worse than what you did."

She chuckled lowly. "I remember. And you're right; I definitely wanted to say something else."

"You are—"

"Well, it's been a pleasure, Commander, but I have to go. Take care of yourself out there." Alexis stepped away from the rail and took a few steps toward the door, not wanting or ready to hear what he was going to say.

"It will be a pleasure," he purred in her ear.

How the hell did he move so fast? She froze. There were two choices here: file a complaint and get him in trouble *or* flirt back. *Girl, like there was any choice!* "What will?"

His hand touched her back, leading her towards the hatch. Unless she opened the thick door, there was nowhere to go except into him if she turned around. "Us."

She turned and looked him directly in the eyes. "Commander, what exactly are you talking about?"

"You know what I'm talking about." His words were smooth.

And she did. But for the life of her, she didn't want to admit it. "No, I don't. I have to get going." She paused with one hand on the handle. "Goodbye, Commander."

Scott's body clenched. He couldn't be angry; she was doing the right thing. He was the one breaking protocol. Scott could be sent for a Captain's Mass and she could get in trouble as well. Yet suddenly, he didn't give a damn. The seven previous times he'd been in her presence, he hadn't done what he'd longed so much to do, so now he had to taste her. Two seconds later, he hauled her up against the solid wall of his chest and his lips were on hers.

His tongue slid around her full mouth before plunging into hers, not asking. Oh, no, he was demanding her acceptance. Her taste was amazing; he couldn't get enough. Every small sample he got increased his desire for more one hundredfold.

Suddenly the handle for the hatch began to move. They sprang apart and leaned on the railing, staring out at the ocean by the time the intruders made it through the opening. Two ensigns looked at him and nodded before leaving. It was obvious what they were up to—nothing so different from what Commander Leighton had planned for the lovely Chief Rogets.

Close on their heels was Alexis. "We aren't done, Alexis," Scott said in his deep tone.

She didn't even turn to look at him, but he saw her shiver just a little. "Take care of yourself, Commander." Then she was gone, leaving him alone. He stayed there even as an hour later he watched the helicopter carry her further away from him against the dusky sky.

Chapter Two

San Diego, six months later...

The bullet wound in his side seemed to be getting worse. *What did you expect, Scott, that it would feel better?* He stumbled down the darkened street knowing he was not of the right persuasion to be down here, but he didn't care.

The sudden lights blinded him and he stumbled to a halt, holding his hand in front of his eyes. As he lowered his hand Scott found himself surrounded by a group of younger men of a variety of races who didn't look at all happy to see him. Their weapons were shoved into the waistbands of their pants and Scott, although extremely fatigued, went into battle mode.

"Well, well, well. What have we here?" one of the men asked his friends.

"I think you took the wrong street, man," another said as a third shoved him to the ground.

Scott showed no emotion as he was forced to the pavement. *Maybe they just want to scare me,* he told himself. The second he felt a kick in his side he knew he was wrong. His body reacted violently as the next person kicked him.

Reaching out, he grabbed a leg and twisted it, tossing the body off balance. As that man hit the ground, the others began to swarm over him. The loss of blood slowed Scott down considerably. The men were obviously high and felt no pain, whereas he did. He was holding his own until he felt a hit into the back of his head and he dropped like a light, losing what little ground he'd gained.

What are they up to now? Alexis hurried towards the group of guys that seemed to be kicking or at least prodding something. Her hair bounced in time with her steps; she'd just left the corner bar from her date and wasn't in the mood for Jay and his gang. They knew better. Last week she'd found them beating a helpless puppy in a bag; their behavior was getting old. "Hey!" she shouted, getting their attention. "Back off," she ordered.

The ringleader looked up and rolled his eyes. "Lex, go home," he yelled back as her steps brought her closer. "It ain't got nuttin' to do with you."

She ignored him and shoved her way through only to stop and gasp. The form on the ground was a man. "What the hell are you doing?" Instantly, she placed herself over the man who was lying face down and began to check him for injuries, each one she found making her angrier. The Caucasian male was either unconscious or very close to it. Checking for a pulse, she breathed a bit easier when she found it, faint but steady. Her body trembled as she touched him.

"Leave him alone! He shouldn't be down here! And we found him like this" the oldest boy protested.

Rising to her full height, she glared back at him, totally unintimidated. "What the hell do you think you were doing? The puppy was bad enough, but damn it, Jay, this is a man."

"He was trespassing. We were just looking to see if he were dead. We didn't beat him up."

Trespassing? The man on the ground moaned. "I suppose he got these injuries by himself? Get out of here," she hissed as she knelt back down beside him. "Easy now." Her voice dropped into her soothing bedside manner voice.

"Alexis?"

Her heart froze. *No, it couldn't be. Not here.* Carefully, she rolled the man over so she could see his face. *Oh, dear Lord. It was.* "Commander?" she asked softly.

"You know him?" Jay asked.

"Get over here, Jay, you and the rest of your friends who seem to think I am not serious. Pick him up and take him to my car." She stood quickly. "Hang in there, Commander." Her eyes snapped with impatience. "Now! Damnit, move!"

The five remaining men struggled to carry him to her sport utility vehicle, before they climbed in at her glare to ride with her to her small, three-bedroom rambler. She led the way to her spare room as the boys carried Scott laid him on the bed.

"Where do you know Casper from, Lex?" Jay asked her.

"He is a Commander in the US Navy and a SEAL, so if you guys weren't getting the shit kicked out of you, then he has another injury somewhere."

"Alexis?" The slur came again.

"I'm here, Commander. Right here." Instantly she was beside him, touching his face. "I have to check you out. Can you tell me where you are injured?"

Those eyes opened and settled on her face. A quirky smile tugged the side of his mouth. "Still so beautiful, I like your hair down. I have a gunshot wound in the side." He looked around the room at the men. "Is it safe here?"

Jay stepped forward. "We'll be the ones asking questions, Casper. Where did you get shot at?"

Alexis waved him away, her insides trembling at Scott's words. "You're fine. You are at my house."

"Them?"

"They helped bring you here. Close your eyes, Commander," she ordered as she moved towards her doctor's bag. "I have to get you stabilized and to a hospital."

"No!" He grabbed her arm, sending shivers through them both. "No hospital."

She removed his hand carefully, ignoring his comment, and got her bag. "Quiet. Conserve your energy."

Scott did, slipping into unconsciousness.

"You gonna call the police, Lex?" Jay asked as he watched her skillfully remove Scott's shirt to expose the gunshot wound. It sat about an inch lower than the scar left from when she'd sewn him up on the *Endeavor* the last time they'd met.

Alexis disinfected her hands with a towelette. "You better pray I don't. You boys would be in serious trouble, attacking a man just because. Don't tell me you are trying to join that damn gang."

Jay turned away from the man's scarred body. There were dark bruises forming from where he and his boys had kicked him. "I swear we didn't shoot him, Lex."

"Quiet, Jay, let me concentrate." There was silence in the room as her now-clean fingers probed into the wound, then she stuck in some clamps and pulled out the bullet. Correction, bullets. There were two inside his flesh. Holding the second one up, she frowned. "Hmmm. It's a .38. Interesting." She dropped it into the metal dish with a loud clang.

Her arresting gaze took in each and every one of the young men in her room. "Think about the choices you make, 'cause I don't want to be doing this to you one day." Her lean hand shook the container holding the bullets. "Now, go on, get some sleep."

"It started to rain, guys…it's gonna be a wet night," Jay told his crew.

"Guys," Lex interrupted. "I meant go crash in the living room. You know you are welcome to stay here. Just make sure you don't disturb him." Five young men smiled at her as they went to grab their usual sleeping gear from her hall closet to make up their beds.

※

The whispering grew louder. Scott opened his eyes and found two men in the room going through the closet. His body tried to react but he felt almost paralyzed.

"He's awake, go get Lex," one of the guys said. The other one disappeared out the door. Dark, distrustful eyes fell onto him.

Scott didn't move, just stared back. Movement at the door caught his attention. It was Alexis. She wore a cream-colored, short-sleeved shirt and a pair of jeans that should have been declared illegal, they fit her so tightly. Even hurt and feeling like this his body reacted to her.

"Morning, Commander, I see you made it through the night." Her eyes flashed with humor.

"You didn't take me to a hospital," he stated the obvious.

"Nope, you didn't want me to and so, against my better judgment…I treated you here." She moved to the bed and her scent filled the deep breath he took. Her hands were professional and steady as she checked the wound. "Gonna tell me how you got this, Commander?"

"Thank you," he murmured as his hand reached for hers.

She froze at his touch. "For what?"

"Finding me."

It was as if there were no one else in the room with them, the tension grew so thick. "About that wound, Commander," she insisted, removing her hand from his. Her gaze was direct.

"We aren't on the ship, Alexis; you can call me Scott," he said.

"I'm afraid that doesn't change who we are *or* protocol, sir."

With an energy he didn't know he had, Scott sat up in the bed, oblivious to the fact he was shirtless. His face got right into Alexis's. "That is where you are wrong. It changes everything." He dropped his voice even more, "Not that it would matter. I'm a SEAL, Alexis, and I do things my way." *And I want you, regulations be damned.*

"Well, I'm not a SEAL, I'm a doctor and it would affect my career." Her words were level and direct.

Nose to nose, they faced off, neither backing down. "Do you really think I would do something to hurt your career?" His hand cupped the side of her face. "I feel how you react to my touch, Alexis, and my body reacts the same way to you."

She swallowed hard. "I don't know you, except that you are an officer...a superior officer...and it is against regulations to have that kind of relationship with you."

He clucked his disapproval. "We aren't serving in the same place. We are both consenting adults and therefore there is no coercion on either part."

"What makes you think that?" She barely breathed the question.

"I have known that since the first day we met." His fingers moved again. "And each time after that. It was only a matter of time." His voice just as low as hers, so although they were observed by the group of young men, their conversation was unheard.

"You seem mighty sure of yourself...Commander."

He nodded slightly. "I am. Just like I know you are dying to say my name, to hear it rolling off your tongue, just like I am. I am very arrogant. I know that and so do you, but you love it." His thumb moved over her lower lip. "You loved how I kissed you standing at the fantail on the *Endeavor.*"

She whimpered, her eyes fluttering as she swayed slightly towards him.

"Don't worry. I will wait to hear you scream my name. That will be as I am sliding my thick, hard length deep inside your body." As potent as liqueur, his voice poured over her. "Alexis, when we make love, it will be like nothing either of us has ever experienced. I can't wait much longer." He dropped his hand as he slumped back on the bed, exhausted. His eyes twinkled as he licked his firm lips, "Nice to know you want me." That blue gaze fell to her chest, noticing her hardened nipples through the shirt.

A loud pounding on her screen door seemed to jolt her back to earth. "Excuse me, Commander." She rose off the bed and walked past the boys who were standing there, watching the whole interaction avidly.

"You can run, my little healer, but be forewarned: there is *no* place for you to hide." His words followed her out of the room and up the hall to where she looked out the door and found the police.

"Can I help you, Officers?" she asked, taking in the two who stood there on the other side of her screen door.

"We are looking for a man who was last seen in this area," the larger of the two cops said.

"Sorry, Officer, you are going to need to be a bit more specific than that. There are a lot of men around here."

His eyes narrowed at her quick retort, but he continued. "He may be injured."

Years of keeping a bland expression on her face came in handy now as she merely said, "And?"

"Can we come in?" the other cop asked.

She shrugged and opened the door, inviting them in. "Can you give me a bit more information about this person you are looking for?"

"Well, he is reported to be tall, muscular, blond..." the officer trailed off as something caught his eye. Alexis followed his gaze and prayed for strength as she saw Scott enter the room chatting with the other boys like he belonged there. "And you are?" the officer asked, taking in the out-of-place white man in the house.

Alexis watched as Scott's broad-shouldered body filled her living room. He wore his shirt, which she had washed and had sewn up the tear in last night so it looked no worse for wear the officers' view. His body looked poured into his jeans and tennis shoes were on his feet. In no way did he resemble the man from whom she had removed two bullets. His blue eyes immediately moved to her as if assessing that she was okay. Touched by his concern, she nodded slightly.

Chapter Three

"Sir, I believe I asked you a question," the smaller officer said.

"What's going on here?" Scott asked, moving to stand closer to the woman he was going to protect for the rest of her life. *That and marry her.*

"We are looking for a man who was injured in this area who fits your description. Can I see your identification, please?" The officer held out his hand.

"Sure, but if you don't know who the man is, then what good is my identification going to do?" He reached into his pocket and pulled out his wallet to get his card.

"You sure are asking a lot of questions. What's your name?" He gestured impatiently for the piece of plastic.

"Lieutenant Commander Scott Leighton," he snapped in return, handing over his military identification. He didn't like the way the men looked at Alexis. *Hell, I don't like any man looking at Alexis. My Alexis.*

"How do you know Ms. Rogets here?" the larger man asked in a snide tone.

Thick arms crossed, showing not one shred of pain from his wound, as a blond eyebrow rose. "Are you trying to imply something, Officer?" He looked at the nametag. "Johnson?"

The officer took a deep breath and tried to look as impressive as Scott, only to fail miserably. "Of course not, it's just that we are wondering what you are doing here."

Alexis shifted closer to Scott. "We are both in the Navy and have," she paused and glanced at him, "served time on the same ship."

Scott looked at the woman standing next to him, her head barely coming to his shoulder. She was ready to defend him. He held out his tanned hand for his ID. The officer returned to him with great reluctance. "I had some business to do around here and came to ask Alexis for her help on it." His eyes dared the men to say anything to dispute him.

Clearing their throats, the police looked at the five young men also in the room and the smaller one, Officer Petrasla, nodded his head at them. "What are they doing here?"

Fists clenching, Alexis took a step forward. "They have every right to be here. They were here last night. This is my cousin and his friends. Are you implying something, now?" Her tone had grown cold.

It was a simple action by Scott, reaching out and touching her shoulder, but it halted her forward movement. "I'm sure," he drawled, "that these officers wouldn't insinuate anything when it is obvious that I am not the man they are looking for and the young men here are not doing a single thing wrong."

Officer Johnson got the hint and shrugged. "Well, if you see him, Ms. Rogets, please give us a call." He grabbed his partner's arm and led him back out the screen door and down to the patrol car.

"What made them come here?" Scott asked once the officers were gone.

"They always come here. I don't always know them but the officers always know me." Alexis looked at the young men in her house. "Well, come on then. Breakfast is ready. Put your things away and get into the kitchen. I have better things to do today than baby-sit you bunch of ragamuffins," she huffed even as she winked at them.

"We love you, too, Lex," the group said as one before they headed for their sleeping bags to put them back in the hall closet.

She grumbled and walked off, just expecting that Scott would follow her. "Well, get yourself some breakfast, Commander, unless it isn't your kind of food."

Scott looked at the sideboard that teemed with steaming food. It looked like enough to feed an army, or at least his SEAL team. His stomach growled as the intoxicating aromas filled his nose.

"Go on, if you want any. Better get it before they get here." Alexis nodded toward the stack of plates.

"And you?" His question fell as he reached for a plate, trying to hand it to her.

"No, I already ate." She shuffled away from him.

His eyes moved slowly up and down her body. "Really?" he asked doubtfully.

"I snacked while I made breakfast." The noise from the boys grew louder.

"Don't you know I know you are lying to me? Trust me; I like a woman who's willing to eat in front of me. Are you back to being scared, Alexis?" he challenged.

She snatched a plate and before she could say a word, he interjected, "Or did you need a good morning kiss?" His mouth was right next to her ear.

He felt her shiver. "I don't think so," she managed to mutter.

"I do." His arm snaked around her waist, spinning her towards his body...and his mouth. Unlike their first kiss on the carrier, this one was gentle. A learning kiss. Scott slipped his tongue into her mouth and stroked it against her own. It was a slow, drugging kiss that left him shaking in his sneakers.

Time stood still for the two as they were locked in an embrace. Scott had one arm around her and her one free arm slowly made its way around his lean waist.

"Uh-hmmm," came the interruption. "Lex, what the hell is Casper doing sucking on your face?"

They moved slowly apart, like snails in winter. Scott drew her bottom lip into his mouth as they separated, keeping her close for a moment longer. "I love how you taste," he whispered as he released her.

"Eat your breakfast, Jay." Her chest heaved as she moved towards the food herself.

"And Casper here?"

"Why do you keep calling me that?" Scott asked.

"Have you noticed your skin color, man?" Jay snapped, taking his plate and making it so Scott couldn't stand next to Lex.

"I get it, Casper, as in the ghost, the *Friendly* Ghost." He moved to the other side of Alexis and ignored the warning glare from her pintsized bodyguard.

"Man, I don't want your lips anywhere near Lex," Jay threatened.

Setting down his plate beside the seat that Alexis had taken, Scott sat down and pinned the young man with a purposefully bland stare. "My relationship with Alexis is not any of your concern."

"Jay, sit down," she interjected quickly. "Commander Leighton and I don't have a relationship other than a working one. What you saw was a mistake and it won't be happening again," Alexis said firmly.

Like hell it won't be happening again. "There you have it." Scott sent Alexis a small shake of his head before dropping it and digging into his breakfast with relish. The relationship was too new for him to hash things out with a young man who wanted to protect her.

As the rest of the group sat down at her long table to eat, talk was turned towards Alexis and her plans for the day. "What gives you boys the right to think you can run my life?" she asked the young men.

"We're family," they responded as one.

"And, yet, you don't stay out of trouble. I can't help you out next time. You know that, don't you?" Her tawny gaze pinned each and every young man there.

"Yes, Lex. We know."

One by one they finished and put their dishes in the sink before kissing her on the cheek and leaving the kitchen. "Dinner's at six-thirty; it's ribs. I'll do some laundry tomorrow as well, so bring a change of clothes," she yelled to their retreating backs.

As the screen door slammed, it dawned on the two adults that they were completely alone. No young people, no crew, no ship, no regulations. Just them. A man and a woman who had a fierce attraction for one another.

Swallowing hard, Alexis shoved back from the table and took her dishes to the sink. She opened the dishwasher and began to load it.

"You can't ignore me forever, Alexis."

She shrugged. "I'm not ignoring you," she lied. "I am just cleaning up."

His chair scraped the wooden floor as he rose with his plate in hand. A glance at the sideboard showed nothing but empty dishes. Those boys had cleaned up every bit of food she'd made for them. "Wow, they sure can eat a lot," he said as he handed her the plate.

"They are growing boys," she replied easily.

"So am I," he muttered as his gaze swept over her denim-covered ass.

Shutting the black door of the dishwasher, she leaned against it and met his blue gaze. "Tell me where you got the gunshot wound." Her tone was doctor-like, demanding an answer.

"There was some kind of shootout a few streets over from where you found me. It was a stray bullet."

Her eyes narrowed. "What were you doing down here, anyway? No offense, Commander, but you don't exactly fit the *look* of the majority of people who come down here."

"Would you please not call me Commander? If you won't call me Scott, call me Harrier. But for the love of God, Alexis, we aren't on any military installation anymore. Don't call me Commander."

"It's easier for me to call you Commander, but I will try to call you Scott for the time being." At his gesture, she took a seat across from him at the table. "What are you doing here? I'm not going to believe you have family down here." She raised a brow quizzically.

The one who I am here to see will be family soon. "I needed to see you."

His blatant statement made her eyes grow wide. "Why?"

He sent her an incredulous look. "Because since I met you in Norfolk, I can think of nothing but you. Jesus, Alexis, I know this will sound corny, but you have bewitched me. Totally."

Alexis shook her head. "We can't do this," came her inevitable protest.

"Don't give me that whole code of behavior or modus operandi shit, Alexis. Where is the nearest military base from here?" At her silence he continued, "See, there is no reason for that to be an issue. You do realize that, although it is frowned upon, people do fraternize in the Navy."

"It may not be a problem for you, being a commissioned officer, but for us non-coms it is. I am not willing to risk my career for a roll in the sack with you, no matter how much I want to, only to have you *need* to put me somewhere where I won't be able to ruin your career, or to please your 'trophy' wife. I worked my ass off at Harvard and I love serving in the Navy, so no matter how tempting it may be…" Her eyes roved over the exposed part of his body as her voice deepened with desire, "And it is tempting, but not worth my career."

His tall body rose gracefully out of the chair and lifted her boldly out of hers, cradling her in his steel-lined arms. He walked to the countertop and set her down, wedging his body between her spread thighs. "I would never," he stated as his hands found the hem of her shirt and moved under it, searching for the skin he knew would be smooth as silk. "*Never* do anything like that to you. I'm not looking for a roll in the hay with you, my little healer. I was thinking something much more permanent than that."

"What do you want from me?" she gasped as his large hands moved up her sides over the lace of her bra.

"I want everything from you." He took a deep breath and moved his hands down out of her shirt and placed them on her sides. "Everything." Then he stepped back and allowed her to jump down from the counter.

"So you took a chance in coming down here, to maybe run into me and what, try out sex with the HMC?" She narrowed her eyes at him. "For that matter, how did you know where to find me?"

He moved towards her again, "I'm a SEAL. That's what I do. And I know you are on leave for the next twenty days." His eyes looked at her directly. "Just like you know all about my file."

"I don't know anything about you, Commander." She was using his title as a barrier.

"Don't start with that shit again, Alexis," his warning came, knowing she was using his title as a barrier.

"I have things to do." The fiery woman stomped off to the living room where she began to clean it up and get it ready for the evening.

Scott followed her. He leaned in the doorway and watched her move around her living room, picking up things and fluffing pillows. "What were you doing over there last night?"

She never missed a beat with her cleaning. "If you must know, I was on a date."

"With whom?" Those two words were growled with such animosity she stopped and looked at him. His eyes were shards of blue ice and there was a very pronounced tick in his jaw.

"That is none of your business." Alexis said with one hand on her hip.

The hell it isn't! "Believe what you will, but you're wrong. It *is* my business. Everything about you is my business."

"So says you," she muttered.

"At least you are beginning to see it my way," came his smart-ass remark. His hard body plunked itself down on the couch she'd just finished straightening as if it were within his every right.

Throwing the pillow she held in her hand at him, she just sat down in a leather chair and watched as he snatched it out of the air, nice and easy-like. "So, tell me what you are doing here, in my neck of the woods?" she asked.

He shrugged a shoulder. "I told you, I came to see you."

"Well, you have seen me."

Not as much of you as I want to. "Take a vacation with me," he blurted out.

"What?"

"Come on, take a vacation with me. I have some down time, at least a week. We could take a cruise," he suggested, then grimaced. "Sorry, I forget you are on the water all the time. A rail ride, spend a few days with me. Get to know me, inside and out."

She sniffed slightly and lifted her chin. "I am on vacation."

"Is this really the vacation you want? Or would you rather spend time with me? I will do whatever you want—anoint you with baby oil, rub you down anytime you want. We can go to movies, whatever. Spend about a week with me, have room service, let me take care of you."

There was a weird, almost glazed look on Alexis's face as she just stared at him silently for a few moments. Then she laughed. "I get it, this is another dream. Very funny, Lex; come on, wake up. As if Commander Leighton would actually come to *your* house wanting to make passionate love to you...no matter how much you wish he would..." she mumbled as she stood and walked back to her bedroom, rubbing her head and totally ignorant of the wide grin on the very real and now very knowledgeable Commander Leighton.

Chapter Four

Scott remained smiling and sitting on Alexis's worn, yet comfortable couch for a minute, basking in the revelation that she wanted him as much as he wanted her, before unfolding his muscled body to follow her.

He bypassed the room he'd slept in the night before and paused at a second. It was wall-to-wall with books: medical textbooks, medical thrillers, Shakespeare, and more. There was a laptop computer on the desk that had a caduceus screensaver floating back and forth on it, changing colors as it went.

There were a few pictures of her naval career on the spaces of the wall not covered by bookshelves. He noticed only one of her family, which was on the top of a bookshelf not in the main line of sight. She had an overstuffed chair beside the window with a stuffed unicorn propped up against the pillow. Leaving the room as silently as he entered, he was left with one other doorway.

Her bedroom. He knocked with one knuckle. "Alexis," he called to her through the door.

Her naturally husky voice reached him. "Come in, Commander...Scott. I am just getting some things together."

Pushing open the door, he stopped and took in Alexis's sanctuary. She had a medium-sized room with two large windows that allowed in the light. A queen-sized bed was against one wall. Everything was neat and orderly.

The colors were subtle and warm of pale purples and soft golds, although her bed was accented by a rainbow of multihued pillows. Her furniture was all dark wood but the somber tone didn't detract from the serenity of the room.

"What did you need, Commander? I can drop you back off at your hotel since I am on my way out. I have to get some more things for tonight's dinner." She was standing in front of the mirror and examining how her shirt looked, totally oblivious to the reaction of the man in the room with her.

Coming closer, Scott looked at her in the mirror. "I'm not a dream, Alexis. I won't disappear if you touch me."

With a swallow she said, "I know you aren't a dream. But I have things to do and I am sure you do as well."

"I want to spend time with you. Get to know you. *All of you.*" He moved even closer to her until his large body stood directly behind her, allowing her to see them together.

She opened her mouth but he reached around her and placed his fingers over her lips. "Don't give me that same speech. I want to spend time with you. Come away with me." His eyes held hers prisoner in the mirror and were full of promise.

"Okay," she said as if a daze. "I can't leave until tomorrow, since I have the dinner tonight." But then panic and shock came across her face.

Oh, no. I'm not letting you out of my sight and giving you the chance to change your mind. I have you now, Alexis. You are mine! "I'll hold you to that," he vowed. The back of his hand ran down the side of her face and she instinctively pressed into it.

"Lex! Lex? Where are you, girl?" The screech reached them all the way back in the bedroom. Immediately, Alexis slipped out of the room, glad for a reprieve from Scott's intensity.

In the middle of the living room stood her neighbor from a few houses up, Shirley Allen, a very happy, very loud, very beautiful black woman. "Hey, Shirl. What's up?" Alexis asked as she approached. *Stay back there, Commander. Please stay back there until she is gone.*

"Well, two things. First off, I hear we are making ribs tonight. Is it going to be a block party?" She waggled her eyebrows at her friend. "You know it's gonna end up as one, so it'll be smart to plan for it from the jump."

"Yeah, you're right. Sure, why not? Spread the word, tell people we eat at six-thirty and the fun begins whenever they arrive." Alexis shook her head as she imagined her night. No quiet evening at home for her!

"Now, Lex, tell me what's this I'm hearin' about some fly-lookin' white Navy officer being here in your house?" Shirley asked in her sly tone.

Alexis felt her whole body blush. "Who told you that?" she hedged.

Shirley ignored that question and pushed for her own answer. "Come on, now, you know damn well I know just about everything that goes on here on this street. Now give!" Arms crossed and one finely plucked eyebrow rose as Shirley waited for the answer.

"There is a guy here I know from the ship. I've seen him around a few times. That's all." She held up her hands and crossed her heart.

"*Umm-hmmm.* And since when you let white men you've seen just a few times stay here? I ain't never seen you let any man stay here. Hell, I ain't ever seen a white man visit you!" Her foot began to tap. "What's going on with you two?"

"Nothing!" she spit out. As Shirley tilted her head, Alexis repeated it in a calmer voice, "Nothing."

That "nothing" went right out the window as her body trembled, telling her that against her most fervent prayers, Scott had returned to the living room. Alexis watched as Shirley's eyes grew wide and moved slowly up and down the large man who stood behind her. Raw appreciation turned to lust and Alexis found herself not really liking the predatory gaze Shirley suddenly wore.

"Alexis." His deep voice moved over her. "I'm ready when you are. Oh, excuse me." His voice turned almost professional. "I don't believe I've had the pleasure." Stunning blue eyes settled on the woman who stood across from him, moving her eyes over him as if he were a tall glass of water and she were in the desert hankering for a long sip of him.

Alexis took over. "Shirley, this is Scott Leighton. Scott Leighton, meet my friend, Shirley Allen."

A low whistle left Shirley's full, dusky lips. "Damn, you are one fine man. And a whole lotta one. Look at all them muscles you got. What do you do?"

His large body moved up beside Alexis, almost touching her but leaving enough space between them so not to cause suspicion. Yet it was still less than the amount he would leave between them on the ship. "It's nice to meet you, Shirley. I do a little bit of everything." He nodded his short-cropped head at her before putting those beautiful eyes back on Alexis.

"What does that mean?" Shirley moved closer with a noticeable sway to her hips.

"I do things all over," his rich voice said, even as his eyes briefly met Shirley's before migrating back to Alexis.

"I bet you do," she replied as her tongue snaked out and over her lower lip. "Are you staying for the party tonight?"

"Yes, and I am looking forward to it." Again his eyes moved to Alexis.

"So am I, now." Shirley blinked and looked back at Alexis. "Okay, Lex, I will spread the word. I am going to go home and find something to wear that will make the rest of you women look...well, look like men. See you later, Navy man." With a brief wave to Alexis she turned around and sashayed her shapely behind right out the door.

"Well, now, she was right friendly." His voice was right beside her ear.

She was acting like a damn ho! "Yes, that's Shirley for you," she ground out.

Moving behind her so their bodies were touching, Scott slid his hands down her arms, over her hips, and back up to lace his fingers by the button on her pants. "Come now, Alexis," he purred. "Don't be jealous. Ever since I met you two years ago there hasn't been another woman who could pull my attention from your beauty."

His touch totally turning her to mush, Alexis found her body leaning back and settling comfortably into his hard one. Closing her eyes and allowing herself to enjoy the moment, she asked skeptically, "And you expect me to believe that for the past two years no woman—not a single long-legged, busty blonde, brunette, or redhead—charmed her way into garnering your attentions?"

He chuckled. "Two years. Two long years with *nothing* but dreams and visions of you. You aren't the only one who has explicit sexual dreams." His tongue swiped along the back of her ear. "If you tell me yours, I'll tell you mine," he offered in a voice that would make the devil give up his kingdom.

"I...I...I don't know what you are talking about," she stuttered.

"You weren't having a dream when you so delightfully told me all about your dreams. At least I am the man you are dreaming about!" He sucked on the sensitive spot behind her ear. "All you have to do is say the word and we both can turn our dreams into reality. Just say my name," he coaxed.

Alexis swallowed, her knees shaking so badly that she was surprised her butt wasn't on the floor. Her mouth was dry from images of her being able to act out her fantasies with the man behind her, who was nibbling on her neck as if it were a sumptuous pastry. "I...I have to get to the store."

One of his hands splayed across her flat abdomen while his other moved to her mouth. His thick index finger slid over the velvet feel of her lips before he separated those lips to slip his digit into her warm, wet mouth.

Instinctively, Alexis drew it in farther, her tongue moving along it as she sucked on it harder. She could feel his erection twitching against her back, telling her insistently what he wanted.

He moaned softly into her ear as another finger slipped into her mouth. The hand across her belly moved down to cup her between the legs. He stimulated her nether region with his constant rubbing motion. "God, I want you, Alexis," he panted into her ear as his own hips flexed against hers.

She didn't respond. Her tongue slid between the two fingers in her mouth before running around the both of them. Lick, suck, lick, suck. Over and over she worked his fingers like they were something much bigger, much firmer in her mouth. Something she wanted to taste so badly.

His hand moved faster between her legs and her hips began to buck, her legs tightening around his wrist, allowing her to ride him firmly. Her tiny moans became audible as she sucked on his fingers harder. Her strong fingers dug into his thighs as she tried not to crumble to the floor.

"Alexis," he groaned. Her body moved faster, telling him she didn't want to stop. He nipped her quickly on the neck before trying again. "Alexis, we have to stop. Someone is walking towards the door." He pulled his hand away from her legs and her mouth, twisting his head to kiss her hard and fast on the lips before moving away from her to sit on the couch.

Flushed, hot, and extremely aroused, Alexis fought for breath as she saw another neighbor walk up to the door and begin to knock. Swallowing hard and pulling on her shirt, she automatically patted her hair into place and walked over to the door, swinging it open.

"Hey, Richie," she said as she licked her lips. "What's up?"

"Lex," he returned. "Wanted to double-check with you about tonight. Make sure Shirley wasn't lying."

She grinned and waved in the handsome black man. "Come on in. Want some tea or something?" Shirley was known to herald a party when there hadn't been one previously.

"Sure that would be—" His words died and she knew what he had seen. Or rather whom.

"Oh, sorry, this is Scott Leighton. Scott, my friend, Richie Grant."

Six plus feet of mouthwatering masculine physique rose smoothly and walked over to them. Scott stuck out his hand and shook Richie's when it was finally offered. "Nice to meet you." His eyes still burned with a passion that only Alexis would be able to extinguish.

"Sure man." Richie looked back at Alexis. "Well, Shirley wasn't lying about there being a white man in your place."

Alexis just headed for the kitchen and poured three glasses of sweet tea. The men walked in the room in silence. Richie thanked her for the drink and all Scott did was wink at her, causing her body to grow damp again.

Propping a hip against the countertop, Alexis looked at the two men in her kitchen. One was about six foot with dark-chocolaty skin, a winning smile, and kind eyes. He kept his head shaven and had no facial hair. His muscular build showed underneath his light-gray muscle shirt and tight pants. Dating a man like him would make it easier on her life; he was a hard worker and one of the *gentlest* men she'd ever met. But she'd never been attracted to him in that way, unlike the other man in her house.

That one was six-five with golden blond hair that he kept in a crew cut. He had almost no body fat on him at all, nothing but rippling muscles. He, too, was clean shaven, and she wasn't sure how that happened since he didn't have access to a razor this morning. His eyes could make her heart skip a beat with their gentian violet-blue color.

Scott was poetry in motion when he moved. His chest didn't have much hair on it, but it was chiseled as if out of granite. In fact, his whole body was. It amazed her how nice it'd felt to be up against all that hardness. As many muscles as Scott had, she would have thought it wouldn't be comfortable to be pressed against him. How wrong she was.

As if he could read her thoughts, Scott found and held her gaze as he took a drink of the tea she had poured for him. Those damn eyes toured her body as if he owned the property rights to her.

Richie drained his tea and took the glass over to the sink, breaking the hold Scott's eyes had on Alexis. "So, Lex, it's a go?"

"Sure is, Richie. Party starts before we eat and we are eating at six-thirty. Like Shirl said, it would turn into one anyway so if we put out the word, others will bring food."

"Gotcha covered. Drinks are on me." He winked at her.

"They better be. I'll see you tonight?" Her hand touched his arm gently.

"I have never missed one of your parties and I will be damned if I start now." He nodded at the man who stood watching his every movement with a calculating look. "Nice to meet you, Mr. Leighton."

"I'm sure I'll see you tonight," Scott stated calmly.

"You're staying for the party?" Richie asked, flicking his eyes back to Alexis. "Lex? He's staying?"

Those blue jewels fixed themselves on her face as Scott waited to hear her answer. Alexis nodded. "Yes, Richie. He will be here. And so, while you are spreading the word, you can also tell them about the commander here. I don't want anyone to disrespect him."

"Commander?"

"Yes, Scott is a commander in the Navy. I call him Commander more often than not. I mean it, Richie, no disrespect. Tell them I mean business."

"Yes, ma'am. I will see you about five-thirty. I will come over and help out with whatever is left."

A brilliant grin crossed her face. "What would I do without you, Richie?" She hugged him swiftly. "Thank you."

Richie leaned in and kissed her on the cheek. "No sweat. See you this evening, Leighton." Then Richie was gone, leaving Scott and Alexis alone in the kitchen for the second time that day.

Alexis looked up and saw the mixed emotions on Scott's face. Those arms were crossed over his chest as he sipped the tea. His gaze fixed firmly on her body, marking her. Claiming her. Setting her on fire.

Chapter Five

Beginning to feel self-conscious, she shrugged her shoulders at him. "What?"

Those blue eyes stayed glued to her darker ones. With a smooth turn of his wrist, he drained the rest of the tea and set the glass down on her marbled counter top. Still silent, his large, muscular body pushed away from the counter he was leaning on and prowled towards her, not stopping until their bodies were less than two inches apart.

"What?" she asked again.

"What is that man to you?" The words were quiet, but the tone was deceptively calm and Alexis wasn't fooled for a second.

"Nothing more than a friend. I have to go to the store. Can I drop you off somewhere?" She took a step back.

"I'm not leaving you, Alexis," his smooth voice said clearly as he reclaimed the step she'd surrendered.

She would love it if he *really* meant that, but she knew that couldn't be true. "Where are you staying?"

His arms reached around her, settling her against his chest and allowing her to hear the beating of his heart. "My bag is at a motel. I want to stay with you."

There have got to be so many rules against what I am doing. "You are free to stay in the guest room tonight. Come with me and we will get your bag, then you can help me with the shopping." She inhaled deeply, utterly affected by the smell of this man.

"Shopping?"

A smile played quirkily on her face as she imagined the horrified look on his. "Surely a big strong man like yourself, a SEAL nonetheless, can handle shopping with a woman," she teased.

"Of course I shop. I do eat."

"I can tell." Alexis pushed back so she could view his magnificent physique. "*Jesú*, Scott what do you weigh, two-twenty?" Her hands moved over his chest and down the side not marred with the bullet wound.

"I thought women didn't like to talk about weight," he said as he looked down at her lissome dark hands moving over his lighter-hued body.

"We don't like talking about *our* weight. You, however, you are a work of art," she breathed. "You must have only three percent body fat, it's amazing." Her hands weren't touching him as a lover would but as a doctor, inspecting and impressed. The light touch moved to one of his arms and trailed up his well-cut arms.

"I weighed about two-thirty-five at my last physical." He grabbed her hands, stopping their movement. "Lex," he groaned. "I haven't quite recovered from the living room earlier, and if you keep touching me like this I promise I will be buried deep inside you in less than five minutes."

"Sorry." Her hands dropped to her side. *He called me Lex. Oh, my God!*

Scott cupped her face. "I love it that you want to touch me; at least we are past you pretending that you don't feel anything for me. But if we are going to get anything done before the party…" He arched an eyebrow, his point made.

"Got it." She smiled and stepped away from his touch. "Let's go. I guess we should get your bag first and then shop." Her feline gaze found his and she narrowed her eyes.

He frowned. "What?"

"How's your wound?"

The smile was masculine and arrogant. "I'll be fine. I have the best doctor in the world."

"That doesn't change the fact I should have taken you in to the hospital," she muttered as she led the way towards the door, grateful he couldn't see the goofy smile she wore on her face as a result of his compliment.

"I'm glad you didn't." He followed her outside and down the steps to her gold Expedition, climbing into the passenger side.

She hopped in as well and followed his directions to where he was staying. Parking at the motel, Alexis turned off the motor. "Well, I will wait here."

"No, come inside. I want to show you something."

I know where that will lead. "I think I have seen everything you have to offer me, Commander," she stated.

He groaned. "Back to that name, are we? And for your information, there is something that you haven't seen of mine. Not yet anyway. Don't worry, you'll like him. And I know he's dying to get to know you." He leaned over and kissed her quickly on the mouth before jumping out and jogging up the stairs to grab his stuff.

Fanning herself, Alexis kept her gaze fixed firmly on the tight ass as it moved out of her sight. Blinking hard, she grabbed pen and paper and began to make a shopping list for tonight's party.

Movement on the stairs caught her attention about ten minutes later. *Dear Lord, that man is fine!* "*Jesú*," she panted to the interior of her car. Down the last few steps walked a vision. He just oozed sexual virility.

Scott had changed. He now wore a white tee shirt and another pair of body-hugging faded blue jeans. Slung casually over his back, as if it barely weighed an ounce, was a sea bag packed full.

Every woman in the vicinity stopped and looked at him in amazement and lust. It filled Alexis with a bit of pride to know that the object of their affection was striding towards her. *Not them, her.* He tossed his bag in the back mere seconds before his immense size filled her vehicle.

"Sorry about that," he said as he shut the door behind him. "I took a quick shower and shaved."

Just what I needed to know. Like my brain doesn't give me enough erotic images of you. Now you tell me you were showering to add to my mental pictures! Her body squirmed on the seat as she tried to sound unaffected. "That's fine. I was just working on the list of things to buy."

He took the list from the floor where it lay and looked over it. "This is a lot of stuff."

"Yep," came her fast response. She steered them onto the road leading them to the supermarket.

Scott sat in silence for about two minutes. "Question."

"Yes, Commander?" Alexis responded as she pulled into the lot at the superstore.

"Lex," he growled, showing his displeasure at what she called him.

"What, Commander?" she growled back.

"Don't call me that."

Turning off the engine, she maneuvered her head so she could stare at him directly. "When you say 'question' like you did, it's an instinctive response for me. My whole life has been following rules and regulations. I can't stop overnight." Alexis climbed out and waited for him to do the same before she locked and walked away from her vehicle.

He fell into step beside her. "Just try, please. I want to hear you call me Scott, and not as an introduction." That blond head bent close to hers as he whispered. "I want you to scream my name as I pound deep into you."

How can he just say things like this? Alexis stumbled and immediately found herself surrounded by arms that would rival Atlas's for strength. "Thanks," she mumbled.

He released her but didn't move back, positioning himself right next to her, close, as if they were a couple.

They entered the air-conditioned store and Alexis grabbed a cart and headed off. "I can do this part, you just put things in," Scott offered as his hands covered hers and his body trapped her between him and the cart. "Unless," he whispered into her ear, "you are ready to let *me* do the 'putting in'."

She shivered and shook her head. "Stop that." Ducking beneath his corded arms, Alexis picked a direction and walked away, willing her legs to stop being so shaky.

Scott behaved for the most part. The cart became extremely full as Scott dutifully followed Alexis up and down each aisle. Her head turned and caught his bemused expression. "What's the matter?" she asked, placing another object in the cart. "Trying to imagine your SEAL team seeing you do this?"

A brilliant smile crossed his face. "I know they wouldn't believe this for a second."

Her topaz eyes narrowed. "Believe what?"

Scott delved one hand into her loose, thick hair, bringing her closer to him with pressure on the back of her head. His firm lips were a hair's breadth away from hers as he purred, "That their stuffy commander was pushing a grocery cart and doing so quite happily. Don't let your mind even begin to go down that other road, Alexis. Not even for a moment."

She knew what he meant and didn't want to deal with that right now. "What do you mean, stuffy?" This time she walked beside him so they could talk.

He chuckled. "I don't know how to have fun, according to my team. I sit at the hotel after a mission instead of going out and getting a woman...or two." His blue eyes cut down to the beautiful brown face of the woman beside him.

She looked at him skeptically. "Right, so you never went out with women?"

"I didn't say that. It's just that my attitude changed." He stopped the cart and loaded the case of bottled water she pointed to.

"Oh, so you went from being fun to being stuffy?"

"According to them, I did." One long finger grabbed hold of her belt loop when she started to walk on, drawing her back to his chest. "Know when that happened?"

Trying to control the shivers racing through her body, all Alexis could do was shake her head. But he didn't say anything, just waited. After she regained some control she asked. "When?"

"Two years ago."

"Doctor Lex," a voice interrupted them. Alexis turned from the blond man in front of her and looked towards the voice. "Girl, I didn't know you were back home. Why didn't you call me? I would have gone out with you last night so you didn't have to go with Ted."

"Isaac," her cheerful voice responded, stepping away from Scott to hug the man who lived on her street.

"Damn, Lex, you just get hotter and hotter every time I see you. How's the doctor and Navy life treating you?"

"Wonderful. I'm very happy." Alexis turned and her eyes fell on the man standing by her cart. His face was once again unreadable. "Isaac, I would like you to meet a friend of mine, Scott Leighton. Scott!" She waved him closer. "This is Isaac. He lives up the street from me."

"Nice to meet you," came Scott's practiced tone as he shook Isaac's hand. When he dropped it, he physically stayed right next to Alexis instead of backing off.

"And you," Isaac replied, looking between Scott and Alexis knowingly. Nodding his head slightly in deference, Isaac smiled at Lex. "I have to go, but I will see you later on."

"You'll be there tonight, right?" her smooth voice asked.

"Of course." He smiled at her again, "A pleasure, Mr. Leighton." Then he and his cart disappeared from sight.

Alexis still had a grin on her face as she turned her attention back to the list. "What are you smiling about?" he asked.

"Just thinking about tonight. Why?"

They had reached the end of the aisle and Scott backed her against the end cap, oblivious to the eyes that were upon them. "How many more men am I going to have to watch put their arms around you and kiss you?"

How am I supposed to think straight when you are this close to me? Her eyes slowly rose to meet his. "You could always leave and you wouldn't have to see me at all." Her hands moved up to rest on his solid chest.

Another step brought their bodies in contact. Desire burned in his eyes as he stared upon her flawless face. "Oh, no. I am taking you away from here tomorrow and then, my sweet little healer, you will be all mine."

"I shouldn't be going anywhere with you, Commander, you are a sup—"

His mouth slanted across hers, stopping the protest before it could be completed. The cart was forgotten as his arms drew her in closer yet, her breasts mashed against him. Scott ran his tongue around her mouth, as if learning everything he could about her taste.

Alexis felt her hands moving up to latch around his neck with a mind of their own. Her tongue matched the almost frenzied stroking of his. The small of her back arched, pressing herself closer to him. *More, more, I want more of him.* Her hands, strengthened by years of setting bones and moving large bodies, grabbed the back of his head, trying to intensify the kiss.

Scott had cupped her firm ass in his hands, his fingers kneading both the denim material and the flesh underneath. The clearing of a throat caused him to slant his gaze sideways. There were quite a few people standing around watching them. Reluctantly, so very reluctantly, he ended the kiss. His hands let go of her butt and moved up slowly to capture her wrists and bring them back down to rest on his chest.

"We seem to have an audience," he murmured before she could voice her displeasure. Alexis blushed and ducked her head. His arms settled around her, making her feel safe. He tugged her closer as she tried to move away. "I don't think that would be wise." He brushed against her, giving her an up-close feel of his raging erection.

She began to laugh. Burying her head deep into his broad chest, she chortled over the absurdity of the whole situation. "I can't believe this."

"What?"

She looked at him. "This. I follow the rules to the letter, but you, *you* come into my life and suddenly I am..." her voice trailed off, not knowing how to finish that sentence.

"Suddenly you are doing what your body wants, instead of what our society stupidly deems correct." His lips met hers again and he was rewarded with both a groan from her and thunderous applause from those witnessing his actions.

Chapter Six

Another hour and a few hundred dollars later found Scott and Alexis loading the last few bags into the back of her vehicle. Scott took the cart back as she shut the hatch and climbed into the driver's seat, waiting for him to return. When he returned, she revved the engine and pulled out the lot.

"I'm already tired, and now I have to go get the yard set up," she moaned in distress.

"Well, I'm all yours, so use me as you will," he said.

Erotic images flashed before her eyes. "I will take you up on that."

"I hope so," he purred in that velvety voice.

"Oh, I plan on it," came her seductive response. "How is your wound doing? I want to check it again when we get home."

"Home? Works for me. It is doing fine, a bit tender, but I've had worse."

Changing lanes, she looked across the interior at him. "Tell me what being a SEAL is like."

"For me?"

"Yes, I know about the training you have to make it through and all that. But tell me about your team." She paused. "If you can."

"I am part of SEAL Team Seventeen. Our nickname is Melagodon, after the prehistoric shark, the fiercest predator in the ocean." She nodded with understanding. "I went for the SEALs immediately after I graduated from Officer Candidate School…hell you know all about OCS. I have never wanted to be anything but one of the most elite the military has to offer. Something my family's money couldn't buy for me—a badge of honor, pride, and accomplishment."

"Well, it is obvious that you got that much done," she interjected.

"You noticed?" he teased her.

"You are a hard man not to notice, Commander," she revealed.

"And here I have been working hard just to get you to talk to me. Why did you always avoid me when we met in the past?"

Alexis sighed; she had just lost control of the conversation. "Honestly?"

"That's the only kind of response I would ever want from you."

She pulled past her driveway and backed into it expertly and swiftly. Alexis stayed silent until they both had bags in their hands and were walking up the steps and heading for the kitchen. "I tried to keep minimum contact with you because I was nervous."

He set down his bags beside hers and walked with her back to the open vehicle. "Nervous of what?"

"You. I don't like to be out of control and around you that is what I feel. I mean reaching my hand into someone's chest to massage a heart doesn't bother me, but talking to you…I sweat just thinking about it."

He shuddered at that image, surprising Alexis a bit. While blood was an unfortunate but very real part of his life, too, the whole heart-massaging thing seemed a bit much for him. Scott took the last bags inside as she locked the car and then followed him. When she entered the kitchen, he gathered her into his arms. "If it is any consolation, you make me get butterflies in my stomach."

"Stop lying." She slapped him on the arm and moved out of his embrace to begin putting things away.

"I'm not." He held up things and she would point to where he should put them. "That first day, in Norfolk, I was running to catch you so I could find out who you were. And then I almost knocked you down. I was so tongue-tied I could hardly apologize to you."

Scott moved towards her and grabbed the hem of her shirt, towing her in close. "Then I touched you as I tried to ask you if you were okay. From that moment on," he murmured as his hand caressed the side of her face. "From that moment on, you gave me butterflies. No one, and I mean *no one*, has ever given me butterflies."

Catlike eyes grew sultry. "I was so ready to cuss you out. But I bit my tongue when I saw your rank. I wasn't a chief yet back then. After you moved away I watched you walk until I couldn't see you anymore."

His nose flared as his eyes began to burn. "So you were lusting after me." The way Scott drawled it there was no question, it was fact.

"Enough that the other times I saw you I had to leave quickly so I wouldn't give myself away. Are you saying it was obvious that I was avoiding you?"

He kissed the end of her nose. "Only to me since I wanted to talk to you. But I wouldn't think that anyone else would pick up on it." Another few kisses. "But on the carrier it was harder. I wanted to cart you away to my room and..." Scott stopped talking and swept her up into his arms to carry her to the sideboard where he sat her on the platform.

"I really need to check that wound of yours, Commander," she whispered against the warm cotton of his shirt.

"It's fine." His hands moved to slide under her shirt.

"No." She pushed him away and jumped off the sideboard. "I need to see it."

He shrugged and with one smooth motion whipped off his shirt, baring that marbled chest to her. "Look away."

Scarcely keeping her eyes from rolling back in desire, Alexis moved towards him. He stood there in nothing but his jeans and shoes, smelling clean and so masculine. "Lift your arm for me," she ordered, wanting to see the movement and range he had on him.

He did. Those blue eyes never left her, just issued her a silent challenge. "Well?"

"Well, what?" Alexis asked, swallowing and trying to get some moisture into her mouth.

"Don't you need to touch me?"

"Not really," she protested. "I mean you did say it was fine." *If I touch him, I will not want to stop.*

"Well, I would feel better if you touched me."

"I bet." Her eyes grew wide at her slip.

"I will be a perfect gentleman. I know we have a party to get ready for, besides...I get you for a whole week." He pinned a glare on her that froze her next sentence. "If you want to argue, I will take you to your bedroom and ravish you until the only word out of your mouth is 'yes'."

"Is that a promise?" she teased.

Those bedroom eyes darkened with lust. "Two years, Alexis, is a very long time," he ground out.

"I wouldn't know about that." *Dear Lord, what let me say that?*

His eyes narrowed. "You'll forget all others before me," he promised. "And there won't be any after me!"

The devil in her woke. "And what is that supposed to mean? Are you claiming you will ruin me for all others after you?"

Scott was back in her face in a half second. "The day there will be another man for you, is the first time the days of the week don't end in 'y'." He pressed a hard kiss to her full lips. "There is no other man out there for you."

Alexis spoke in a low voice. *"Yo hablo Español. Por lo tanto, para mí, los días no necesitan una 'y'."*

"What?"

"I said, 'I speak Spanish, so for me, the days don't need a "y".' In fact none of the days end in that letter."

He arched an eyebrow. "Meaning?"

"Meaning, Commander, while I agreed to spend time with you, that doesn't give you any rights over me."

His eyes softened. "I know that. This does." Before she could blink, he lifted her body, spread her legs to encompass his hips, and covered her mouth with his. One hand settled under ass, keeping her pressed tight against him, while his other hand massaged the back of her head as he devoured her.

Alexis responded immediately, giving everything she had to the kiss and more. Her legs locked themselves around his waist as her hands held his head. Thick black hair fell around them, cloaking them in the gentle smell of heather, as their tongues dueled for supremacy.

For five minutes they stayed like that until Alexis dropped her hands and moved them all over his torso, inadvertently coming in contact with his fresh wound. He drew away from her mouth with a hiss. "Damn!"

Struggling to get free of his grip, Alexis demanded, "Let me look." Trying not to wince, he held his arm away from his body as she inspected the damage. "I'm so sorry about this," she apologized.

"Don't worry about it."

Getting to her feet, Alexis had to swallow to control the fire this man set to her blood. "I really have to start getting things ready for tonight."

"What can I do?" he asked as he covered up that gorgeous chest.

Make my fantasies come true. Every single last one of them. "Come with me."

Silently he followed her out to the backyard and whistled. This is much larger than I expected."

"It's 'cause I have a corner lot." She waved towards the tables. "Can you wipe them down and put on the tablecloths?"

"Consider it done."

They set up for the party, working well side by side. Scott seemed to touch her body at every opportunity he could, keeping her at a fevered pitch.

"I'll be back, I'm gonna go change," Alexis announced with a slight shiver after he'd walked by and run his hand lovingly across her ass.

"Okay, I'll keep an eye on the grill."

"Thanks. People should be arriving soon so I won't be long." Alexis disappeared into the house.

Scott sat down at one of the tables and was lost in thought when he heard a voice say, "Hey, Casper."

The comfortably lounging man turned his head to see Jay and his friends walk in through the open gate. "Jay, guys," he responded as he stretched out muscular legs and placed well-defined arms on the tabletop behind him.

"Thought you'd be gone by now," Jay hinted with more than a bit of malice. His friends walked up onto the back porch and began to set up the music.

"Guess you thought wrong," the easy reply came.

Dark eyes narrowed as Jay began to puff out his chest and his attitude got colder. "I don't want you here. Lex, don't need you sniffin' around, so just go back to wherever you're from. Go get your jungle love somewhere else."

Storm clouds began to gather in the depths of those cornflower-blue eyes. "Is that what you think I'm doing?" Although he didn't like the implication Jay was making, Scott was pleased that Lex had someone to protect her. *However, now that's my job, kid, so back off!*

"Why else would you be here?"

"Sit down." Scott nodded at the table that was close to his.

"No, don't wanna," Jay snapped resentfully.

In a voice that scared all those hearing it by its lack of emotion, Scott spoke again. "I said, sit down." He never raised his voice; it just grew colder than ice.

Swallowing, Jay did as he had been told. He glared at the white man sitting at his cousin's table. "I'm sittin'. What you gonna say, Casper?"

"First, what goes on between Alexis and me is none of your business. I think it's great you want to protect her. But don't...*don't*...ever try to strong-arm me. Second, I know what you and your friends did to me. You can give me the money back and we will forget it happened."

Jay started to protest, but a shake of the blond head kept him silent. "If you lie to me, it will only make it worse. Just give it back to me and no one will have to know. I don't like being kicked when I am down and I don't like people lying to me. You play hard at being a man, so act like one." Scott leaned forward to rest thick forearms on his thighs.

The young man nodded. "All right. But tell me why you are after my cousin."

"I like your cousin and have since the day I met her in Norfolk." His eyes were direct as he spoke.

"I don't want her hurt or in trouble. You dig me, Casper?"

"I have no intentions of hurting her and I would do nothing to get her career in trouble," Scott answered. *I will just have to make sure we aren't in the same command.*

"Not the trouble I was talkin' 'bout. I'm talkin' 'bout the one that comes along about nine months after you go just a bit farther than you were trying to in the kitchen today."

A kid! What would our child look like? "I don't think either of us is ready for children."

"Well, just so you don't want her money. She's a doctor, but she ain't rich."

"I don't need her money. I have plenty." He cocked an eyebrow. "Anything else you have to say to me before she comes back out?"

"When are you leaving?"

"Tomorrow."

"Good." Jay walked off.

Scott sat alone, lost in a stare at the grill, and his thoughts returned to the time he was in the Belizean jungle and he'd asked his friend Tyson if he were ready to deal with an interracial relationship in the States. Tyson had seemed so sure. Scott knew he was sure, but what about Alexis? Was she?

"What's the matter, Commander? You seem mighty pensive. Come on, loosen up! The party is about to begin." Alexis's rich voice broke into his memories.

With a smile his head turned to her and he froze. *Holy shit, look at her!* "Wow," he breathed as he rose fluidly to his full height. "You look…incredible."

Half of her mouth gave him a smile. "It's just an old dress."

"If that is old, then it is a good thing you are a doctor because when I see you in a new one…I'm gonna need CPR." He took her hand and bowed low over it before kissing her knuckles as his eyes sent her molten promises.

Alexis blushed. Scott held her hand and twirled her around for a better look. Her dress was greenish-blue in color, falling to just below her knees. It flowed about her with every step she took. The straps were wide and offset on her smooth shoulders. It was low-cut in the back, stopping right above her tailbone.

Her hair was gathered back from her face and cascaded down her back in thick waves. Her skin was soft and supple and he could smell the fresh heather as she twirled under his arm. On her feet she wore flat sandals so she could walk on the grass with ease.

Before he could say anything else, around thirty people flowed in through the gate. Within moments the place was blaring with music, food was cooking on the grill, and people were talking and laughing. Most of the time Scott was included; the guests went out of their way to make him feel welcome, but the times he was off by himself his gaze always found its way to Alexis.

Her sparkling personality shone. It was evident to all that she loved them and was well-loved in return. Comparing this woman to the professional one he knew from the Navy, the differences were astounding. Here she was free, exuding life. He loved it. Or was it her that he loved?

The music switched to something slower and Scott found himself looking directly at the woman he'd been observing all evening. "Come on, dance with me?" her sultry voice asked as her hand reached out to him.

Unable to resist her haunting eyes, Scott stood and walked with her to where the others were dancing. Inhaling her gentle fragrance, he fit her into his body as they barely moved on her lawn. Her head fell to rest on his shoulder as slim arms slid, carefully to avoid the wound, around to settle on his back, fingers splayed and gathering him in tight.

"Thank you," she whispered for his ears only. "Thank you for dancing with me."

Chapter Seven

It was close to midnight when the party wound down. Jay and his crew were the last to leave and as they went through the gate, closing it behind them, Alexis surveyed her backyard beneath the outdoor torches that still burned.

"Damn, I'm tired," she moaned to the cool night air.

"That was one hell of a party." Scott decided as he gathered some discarded plates and threw them in the nearest garbage can.

"That little thing? Oh, this was not a big one, which is good. I'm beat." She sat down on the tabletop, hanging her legs over the edge to dangle freely.

"You want to clean up in the morning, then?" he asked as he dumped more things in the trash.

"No, I don't want any animals to start sniffin' around." Her head tipped backwards, exposing her elegant neck to his gaze.

She thought she heard him growl. "Well, then, don't you think you should help me instead of sitting there and tempting me?"

Oh, if only that were true, Commander Leighton, if only that were true. "Right," she complained and started cleaning once more.

Under the muted light of the tiki torches and lanterns her backyard began to take shape. The air was cool with the faint breeze that blew. It also kept the bugs away. Alexis rolled up the last tablecloth and all the discarded cutlery and dishware she'd found and put on the disposable tablecloth. "There is a trashcan right behind you," Scott said, as he tied off the bag in the one he was dealing with.

Cramming the bundle of paper and plastic into the overflowing bin, Alexis put the top on and retreated to her now-clean tabletop for a seat.. Slow, sensual jazz played faintly in the yard, loud enough for her to hear but not loud enough for the neighbors to complain. From beneath narrowed lids, she watched the muscular man on the other side of her yard. Even injured he moved with a panther-like grace that took her breath away.

Her mouth going dry, she lay back to focus on something that didn't have blue eyes, a heart-stopping smile, or a body that could give her an orgasm just by looking at her: The stars in the black night sky. This was something Alexis loved about being on the ocean, the clear, unimpeded view of the stars. If she were to do things again and couldn't for some reason be a doctor, she would have chosen a career dealing with astronomy—maybe being an astronaut. Lost in her thoughts, she just lay there, not knowing how beautiful she appeared to the man in the yard with her.

※

Snapping the lid on the last garbage bin, Scott looked up and nearly dropped his jaw. Lying on her back on top of the table was the object of his dreams. Alexis's legs, bare from mid-thigh down, hung over the edge at her knees. Strong but slender arms were stretched out over her head.

It was like she was just asking him to come over to her. That sweet, succulent body of hers called to him and he didn't want to ignore the cry. Wiping his hands on his pant legs, he swallowed and tried to get rid of the butterflies that were growing in his belly.

Moving slowly, he blew out all the torches and lanterns except the one by the back door, causing her body to fall into the shadows. He knew where she was, though. His body had a radar lock on her position.

As silently as he had been trained to be, he moved in close to her prone body. He watched as her eyes moved across the expanse of outer space. On her face was a contented little smile.

Without speaking, he climbed up onto the table and stretched out next to her. His arm eased its way under head so she was on his shoulder. As if she had been doing it for years, her body curled into his. One of her legs slid over his denim-covered one. A hand found its way to rest upon his chest as his arms encircled her shoulders, totally enclosing her body in his embrace.

Their scents intermingled with the fresh smell of a new day. As he lay there holding her, Scott came to a realization; while he wanted to join their bodies and make them one, he was extremely content to just hold her too. His contentment was such that the noise of the city faded into the background.

"Tired?" He broke the silence with his whisper.

"Very." Her head snuggled in closer to his secure body. "I thought vacations were supposed to be relaxing. I get less sleep on the ship and don't feel this exhausted."

He laughed softly. "Don't worry. I will make sure you get some sleep. Of course, you will be too exhausted to do anything *but* sleep." His lips caressed the smooth skin on her forehead.

"We are getting separate rooms, wherever we are going," the hushed protest came.

Like hell we are. "Oh, no, I can't get to know you if you can lock a door in my face."

"Tell me again why I agreed to this?"

"Because," he said in an intoxicating voice. "Despite what you tell yourself, you want to come with me."

"Is that so?"

"That and for this reason." His fingers tipped up her chin to allow her lips to meet his descending ones.

This kiss, like the others, was a masterful one. His hand stayed against the smooth expanse of her cheek as he deepened the kiss. Their bodies began to roll towards each other, trying to get closer.

Scott pulled away. "I'll be damned if I make love to you for the first time on the top of a picnic table. Make up your mind, Alexis, if it is going to be tonight or not," he ordered with a raspy voice.

"I can't. I'm sorry." Ripping herself out of his arms, she tried to run, but his incredible reflexes caught her before she got more than two steps away from the table.

Pressing against her back, Scott made sure the table was in front of her so she couldn't go anywhere. "Don't apologize, Alexis. I don't want you to feel forced into anything. I can wait. I've waited two years for you. Another night isn't going to kill me. Too much." His mouth nibbled along her exposed collarbone.

"This is going against everything that I have ever been taught," she moaned in despair. "I don't know what to do."

Blue eyes narrowed. *I don't like the sound of this.* "What are you talking about? This is more than just the fact that you are a chief and I am a lieutenant commander in the Navy, isn't it?"

"Yes," fell her soft answer.

He spun her around so her body was facing his. "Close your eyes."

They narrowed instead. "Why?"

"Please. Close your eyes." His hands dropped from her shoulders.

With a shrug she complied. "Now what?"

"Just feel." His callused hands cupped her face. His touch and his voice drowned out everything else around her.

He unpinned her hair, sending all of it tumbling around her head and shoulders. Scott combed his fingers through the thick silkiness of it. Eventually it was pushed away from her shoulders so it all cascaded down her back.

He skimmed her soft eyebrows with the pads of his thumbs. Drifting them down over her eyelids, his touch was ever so gentle. One finger ran down the bridge of her nose and off to the side where it covered her cheek.

His hands were entirely back on her face as his thumbs moved tenderly over her full lips, first the top and then the bottom one. The other fingers trailed down the expanse of her cheeks as his hands moved to her neck. Her body trembled under his loving touch.

"You are a beautiful woman," he murmured into her ear, moving behind her. Strong hands barely made contact with the silken skin of her shoulders until they reached the straps of her dress. One thick finger slid under each strap and glided up and down the smooth material.

The hands moved on, tracing the muscles in her arms as they scarcely touched her skin, but they touched it more than enough to ignite the flames in her blood. His head dipped and Scott began to lick along her collarbone, delving into the hollow of her neck until her whole body quivered.

Scott caressed up her arms and down the sides of her curvaceous body. "I love every inch of this body of yours. Every curve you have was made to fit perfectly into my body." His hands moved over her hips and down the tops of her thighs. "So muscular and yet so feminine."

His hands slid up under the dress, allowing their skin to connect. "Smoothness and softness to rival the most expensive silks and velvets." Higher and higher his hands rose, exposing her legs to the night air. Soon the dress had bunched up around her waist and his hand was heading for the apex of her thighs.

"Tell me something, Alexis."

"What?" she whimpered.

"Are you seeing color now?" His fingers traced the edge of her underwear.

He felt her shudder. "No," she breathed. "I'm not. Even though my eyes are closed, all I know is that I want to be with you. Completely."

"Then open your eyes." She did. His touch was still driving her crazy but as her head turned towards him, he stopped. Dropping the dress back down and moving his arms up to encircle around her. "And now?" he murmured, as she could see his face.

"It still doesn't matter," she murmured.

He nodded with relief. *Thank God.* "Good," he replied as his lips captured hers in a loving and gentle kiss.

"Let's go to bed," she offered.

"Good idea." He picked her up and carried her inside the house, stopping only to blow out the final torch.

At her doorway, he set her down and kissed her again. "Goodnight. I will see you in the morning. We need to leave by noon." Another kiss and he slipped into the guest room and closed the door behind him. That was one of the hardest things he'd ever done in his entire thirty-seven years of life.

Alexis stared in shock at the empty spot where, mere seconds ago, a man whom she wanted terribly had stood. He left her; he actually left her there. *Why am I so freakin' angry? I have been spouting off about the UCMJ, not him. Damn the Uniform Code of Military Justice. Why can't I just take what he's offering?*

"Well, hell!" she swore as she went into her room and kicked off her sandals, letting them land wherever, a trait not her norm. Alexis had never wanted a man more in her entire thirty-four years. Her body had gone *way* past damp the second he'd laid next to her on that table outside. Her legs still shook from the feel of his hands touching her body as she stood there with her eyes closed.

Admittedly, she'd felt very exposed and vulnerable. As his quest had continued, however, all she could feel was the passion he felt for her, the raw desire in his voice as he spoke softly in the night air.

"Damn, damn, damn, damn!" She tossed her dress over a chair as she slid on a pair of short, crimson Harvard boxers and a gray, spaghetti-strap tank top. Before she talked herself out of it, her bare feet had carried her still-throbbing body out the door of her bedroom and straight into his.

Without knocking, Alexis just barged right into the room, the door slamming into the doorstop. "Who in the hell do you think you are, Commander? To treat people like that?" she raged. "Or is it just me?" Stepping to the left, her toffee hand reached for the door and shut it behind her with the force of a gale wind, and then she stopped dead in her tracks.

Scott sat up against the headboard watching her with his hands behind that blond head, that perfect chest of his bare and bathed by the light from the only lamp lit in the room. Her gaze noticed the white sheet drawn up to his waist as well as the jeans that lay folded on the chair. For all she knew, he was totally naked beneath that sheet. *Oh, God, naked...*

His gaze met her angry one calmly. "And how did I treat you, Alexis? You made it clear we weren't sharing a bed tonight. I thought I had been respectful," he said coolly.

"So you never expected to be in my bed tonight? Even when your hands were running over my body?"

"Expect? No." He lowered his arms to rest by his side. "Hoped? Oh, hell, yeah!" Scott looked at her for a moment in silence. "Lex, I know without a doubt that we will make love. The sparks between us are too overpowering to ignore. But I have never nor will I ever force or coerce a woman into my bed. When you say no, it is no."

Feline eyes narrowed with disbelief. Alexis took slow deliberate steps towards him in the bed. "I thought you didn't want me anymore after you left me at my door." She quietly confessed as she dropped to her hands and began to crawl up the bed towards him.

Scott swallowed hard. His direct gaze was glued to the breasts he saw hanging free inside her skimpy shirt. "Just for the record, I left you by your door to show consideration for you. Not because I didn't want you."

Her gaze grew as sultry. "So, am I allowed to change my mind?" Her hips were centered right over his pelvic area and her sweet breath warmed his chest as she prowled closer.

His hands clenched in the sheet that kept his lower body from touching hers. "Don't, Alexis," he groaned. "You made your choice. I'm not a little boy. I don't want to play games."

Her tongue snaked out and licked up his sternum. "I am done playing games, Commander," she purred as her mouth drew even with his. "I can't lie to you and pretend that I don't want you. But you're right, I did make my choice. The wrong one, but at least I know where my mistake was and therefore I know how to fix it."

Scott closed his eyes, as if praying for strength.

"Look at me," she said against his mouth. He opened his eyes, dark with longing. "*Bésame*, Commander," she ordered.

Scott might not have known what she said, but he got the idea. His hands moved up and, as his fingers gathered fistfuls of her silken hair, he pressed his lips to hers, sliding his tongue deep into the welcoming warmth of her mouth.

Alexis immediately whimpered as his tongue plundered hers. Moving her lower body up more, she straddled his lean hips and sat down on his lap so her hands could slide around the back of his head and hold him as he held her.

Each of them explored the other's mouth. Eyes drifted closed as souls were joined. Keeping their foreheads pressed against one another, Alexis released his mouth and just sat there with his strong hands intertwined her hair, his erection pressed up between her legs, the scent of Scott all over her and her kiss-swollen lips aching for more of his gentle yet masterful touch.

"I know I made my decision, but I don't want to be alone tonight," she confessed in a small voice.

"And you don't have to be," came his gravelly response. "You don't have to be."

Slipping into the bed on the side of him that wasn't injured, Alexis felt a peace surround her that she hadn't ever been aware of before. Security and contentment. As he turned off the light and gathered her against his protective body she sighed deeply. "Thank you," she murmured as the days events overtook her and she feel asleep.

"Sleep well, my sexy sienna healer. Sleep well." With a kiss to her head he, too, slept.

Chapter Eight

"Why won't you tell me where we are going?" Alexis protested as the driver put her bags in the trunk of the cab. She climbed into the backseat ahead of the blond-haired, blue-eyed man with her.

"Don't you think that defeats the whole idea of a surprise?" he responded with a chuckle.

"Humph." She slid across the leather seat so he could climb in on the same side, and tried to ignore the fact that her neighbors were watching avidly.

"Come on, now. You'll love it, I promise," he coaxed for a smile and was rewarded with one. His gaze also took in the ogling stares but they didn't seem to affect him at all.

Closing the door he smiled as the taxi drove them away from prying eyes. He looked at the woman beside him. Meeting his eyes, she fell victim to his cornflower-blue orbs. "Where are we going?" she tried again.

"These lips are sealed," he answered with a wink.

Alexis looked down at herself. She wore khaki capris and a black sleeveless shirt that displayed her well-toned arms. On her feet was a pair of black sandals that showed off the French manicure on her toes. Her hair was loose, framing her face, softening her appearance even more. "How can I be sure I packed the right clothing?"

Scott shook his head. "Not gonna work. I was with you as you packed so you have the right clothes."

"Fine," Alexis huffed, crossing her arms over her chest.

"You're very adorable when you pout, did you know that?"

"I'm not pouting."

He shrugged. "Okay, but I still think you're adorable."

Adorable. That one word made her feel like the only woman in the world. "Will you do something for me?"

"What is it?" He moved his burning gaze up from her chest to her face.

"Teach me some self-defense moves."

His eyes turned stormy. "Who's threatened you?" The menace in his voice caused even the cabbie to look at him in shock with a bit of fear.

She immediately reached across the cab and laid a dark hand on his solid arm. "No one. I just want to learn." At his skeptical look, she reiterated, "No one has threatened me."

"Alexis," came a deep rumbling growl.

"I promise, Commander, no one has threatened me." She began to move her arm back and he grabbed hold of it and skated her body across the smooth seat to anchor her next to him.

"You will tell me if anyone does." It was another order, not a question.

"I don't need you to protect me."

"Maybe not, but *I* need to protect you." His knuckles skimmed over her cheekbone. "I want your promise, Lex," he rumbled.

"Okay, I promise. I will let you know if anyone threatens me." She shook her head in dismay as she spoke.

He opened his mouth to respond verbally but stopped. Any further protest was halted as the cab pulled up to the airport loading/unloading zone to stop by the door for their airline.

"A flight?" Alexis watched as her bags were whisked away by an attendant at Scott's order.

"You're not afraid to fly, are you?" he asked as he slid his arm around her back and escorted them inside the cool airport.

"No, I'm not." Her brows furrowed as she wondered what was in store for her.

"Don't worry so much. We aren't leaving the country. Does that help?"

"A bit. There's gonna be access to a phone if my...our pagers go off, right?"

A low growl slipped from him as if annoyed by the prospect. "We have our cells." He began to laugh. "I'm not taking you to bum-fuck-Egypt, you know. There will be civilization, precooked food. We aren't going to be roughing it. I *did* say vacation."

Alexis narrowed her gaze at the brunette trying to make eye contact with her handsome traveling companion. "Good," she said. "'Cause I am going to expect what you promised. Especially the massage. I can't wait to have a handsome masseur rubbing down my weary body."

Spinning around to face her, Scott hissed, "I'm gonna be giving you a massage if you want one." His eyes were narrow slits.

Alexis gave a half shrug. "Whatever." Inside she was dancing a jig. *He couldn't care less about that cute dark-haired woman who had been flirting with him!*

Jerking her up against his firm body, Scott kissed her hard and fast. "No, not 'whatever.' Nice to know you were jealous." His words were whispered. "But why would I want that when I have the most attractive woman in the world right here in my arms?"

"I'm not jealous." *Liar.*

"Liar." Another kiss before he released her and moved them up in the line.

Alexis remained silent as he got their tickets. A bit nervous now, she followed him through the security checkpoint. Maneuvering through the people, his question reached her. "What's keeping that brain of yours working so hard?"

She glanced sideways at him. "Just thinking."

"About what?"

"Nothing specific, just odd and random thoughts."

"Trust me, Lex," came his seductive timbre as he turned her head toward him to allow his lips to brush over her forehead. "Please trust me."

Her eyes fluttered closed at the feel of his lips on her skin. "I do trust you, Commander. If I didn't, I wouldn't' be here with you."

"Will you stop calling me Commander? All it does is keep reminding us both of our respective Naval ranks."

"I don't think I will ever forget you are my superior officer."

"I don't want to be the 'superior officer' this week, Lex. I want to be your friend." His hand cupped her cheek. "I want to be your date and I want to be your lover. I just want to be a man who is taking *his* woman on a trip."

Be your lover. Be still my beating heart. "No matter how hard you try, you will *never* be 'just a man'. Even though we are on leave, it still doesn't change who we are."

His hands moved to her shoulders and gave her a little shake. "We aren't even in the same damn command, so it doesn't matter." Suddenly gentle, his thumb caressed her full bottom lip. "From now on, call me Scott." His eyes begged for her compliance.

"I'll try."

"Thank you. Now let's get on our plane." His hand grazed over her butt as she turned and began to walk away.

"Hey, now," she protested as her insides melted. "What was that for?"

"Would you believe I couldn't help myself?"

"Not for a second," she retorted.

Thirty minutes later they boarded the plane. As she checked her belt, her gaze took in the man beside her. He wore white tennis shoes, another pair of his jeans that never ceased to raise her blood pressure, and stretched across that impressive chest of his was a cobalt-blue tee that outlined every rippling pectoral that lay beneath the cotton.

Everything about him drew her gaze hungrily. "First class, huh?" she said, trying to keep her thoughts from traveling into sexual fantasy land. *A bit late for that, Miss Missy!*

"Of course." He took two glasses of champagne from the attractive flight attendant. "Here you go." He offered her one of them.

"Trying to get me tipsy, Com...Scott?"

"Not yet," he drawled with a grin. A grin that faded as he spied another man in first class eyeing Alexis.

She sipped from her drink. "What's wrong?"

"Nothing," he grumbled.

"Why are you scowling?"

"No reason. I'm sorry."

"Hey," she responded with a wave of her elegant fingers. "You put me in first class and give me alcohol, I'm good. Scowl all you want."

A smile broke through the scowl. "You're amazing, Lex."

She winked at him. "Nice to know you're jealous." Alexis toasted him with her champagne flute. "Don't try to deny it. Every time that man two rows up turns around, your whole body gets stiff."

He merely shrugged. The plane took off and for the four and a half hour flight he held the hand of the woman sitting with him. They began to get to know each other by talking about their childhood.

※

Scott drove the car into the garage of the house that sat right along the beach.

"Where are we?" Alexis asked as she got out and inhaled the smells of the ocean.

"My family's beach home."

She whistled through her teeth. "Wow." It was a huge three-story home made out of marble. "This is your beach home?" *I don't want to stay here.*

"Yes." His skin held a hint of blush to it. "We are just here to get the keys for the cabin that is further up the beach. Too many of the family comes here and I don't want to be disturbed with you."

Or you don't want them to see me.

"Don't even think that. I will introduce you to my family, but not on the first day of our vacation. We will get settled in first."

Her eyes grew wide as she looked at him. Had he heard her?

"Your thoughts were all over your face. Oh, Lex," he swept her back against the cool marble pillar of the front porch. "I want to be with you. Stop thinking that I would let someone insult you because of your beautiful toffee skin. I am so proud to have you beside me."

"Can we talk about something else?" She wasn't quite ready to deal with this yet.

"I just have to grab the keys. They are right inside the door. Coming?"

"I'll just wait right here. Would it be okay if I went down to the water?" Her hands rested against his shoulders as she met his gaze.

"Sure, I'll come get you when I'm done inside." He sent her a smile as he ran his hands up her arms to brush over her face. "Thank you for coming with me."

"I will meet you on the beach." She ducked her head as she slipped from his embrace.

"Lex," his rich voice called.

Looking at him over her shoulder through the thick hair that covered one eye she waited for him to continue. "Yes?"

"Miss me." He winked and slipped in through one of the massive double doors.

Not even containing her laugh at his not-so-subtle order, Alexis moved easily down the path that led to the beach. How she loved the ocean. Slipping off her sandals, her steps took her closer to the breaking waves.

She didn't know which one she preferred more, the Pacific or the Atlantic Ocean. They were both amazing in their own right. The Atlantic had the sunrise while the Pacific had the sunset, and both could make her weep at their beauty.

Alexis moved into the cool water, allowing the gentle waves to lap at her legs. She just stared out to sea.

Harrington Prescott Broderick Leighton, III stood on the edge of the beach and looked at the woman who stood in the water. Her fingers trailed in the liquid and she seemed unconcerned with the fact that the legs on her capris were wet. He'd passed her discarded sandals on the way down here.

"Could I be falling in love?" he asked no one in particular. "What does this one woman have over me that makes it impossible to get her out of my head? She is so beautiful, but I have no idea what to do."

He'd removed his shoes and socks and placed them where he'd seen hers. With a glance at his pants, he shrugged and moved silently into the water. Slipping up behind her, he slid his hands around her waist and placed a kiss on her temple.

"Mmmm. You should be careful, sir. I don't normally let strangers kiss me."

"Well, I am grateful that you have allowed me to, my ebony enchantress." His hands went under the hem of her shirt and teased her flat stomach. "I would have another, if I can turn you from whatever man holds your affections."

She smiled as she overlooked the ocean. "What makes you think any man holds my affection?"

"So no one does?" His hands moved down to run over her thighs.

"I didn't say that. I just asked what made you think that any man held my affection."

"Tell me about him," he ordered.

With her head resting against his shoulder Alexis put her smaller hands over his forearms. "There is nothing to tell."

"So, are you unattached?" His breath warmed her ear.

"Well, there is this one man…" She let it hang.

"And?"

She looked at him over her shoulder. "And nothing. That man will be by the wayside if he doesn't feed me, 'cause I am hungry."

His chest moved with his chuckle. "Okay, let's get going. I want to get us settled and then we will go for dinner. I don't have food in the house so we will also have to go shopping."

"Sounds like a plan." She didn't move, just stayed there in his comforting embrace.

I am. I am falling in love. "Let's go."

She sighed heavily but still turned and walked with him back to the car where they slid with wet legs onto the seats. Alexis set her shoes beside her and watched as Scott wiped off his feet and put his shoes back on.

He put them on the small two-lane road that curved with the coastline. It took about twenty minutes of drive time but the scenery was breathtaking. Scott pulled into the paved driveway of a beautiful log cabin.

"*Jesú*, this is your cabin?"

"What do you think?" He put his gaze on her face and waited while she looked around.

The cabin had two stories and there were large, open windows all around that allowed the sun to flood the interior with its warmth and let those inside gaze at the ocean. It sat on a small edge and as they walked towards the door, Alexis saw the path that would take her down to the beach.

"I think it is beautiful. My God, why would you ever leave this place?" she said with awe.

"This is where I come to relax after a mission. Let me give you the grand tour." His hand settled familiarly on the small of her back as he unlocked the door and allowed her to enter first.

Chapter Nine

Coming down the polished stairs, Alexis could only shake her head. This place was amazing. Scott had all modern appliances and technology but the place still retained a comfortable rustic feel to it. The upstairs had five large rooms, the most amazing being the master bedroom where he'd placed their bags.

The room had totally screamed "man". There wasn't a lot of color and the furniture was dark but the room was spotless. His closet was organized as were the rest of the things she spied. His room had a California king-sized bed that was covered with a charcoal gray comforter.

The furniture he had was simple yet functional. There was a straight back chair and a large stuffed armchair beside a small table in his bedroom; this man was not a man for knickknacks. Her eyes grew heavy as she imagined what it was going to be like sharing that bed with him tonight.

"What did you think?" he asked as he met her at the bottom of the stairs.

"I think it is obvious you are a military man; your room is perfectly squared away," Alexis murmured with admiration.

His large hands lifted her with ease off the stairs and he lowered down the hardened expanse of his body. "I love this place," he said in his seductive timbre.

"It is absolutely beautiful. I love this view you have." She squirmed out of his arms and walked over to the front room that overlooked the ocean. The windows were floor-to-ceiling, allowing for a remarkable observation of the brilliant oceanic picture. "It is very easy to see why you would want to come here. Do you spend family gatherings here?"

His body moved up behind her as his arms slid around her waist. Together they stood in the afternoon's fading sun looking out over the vibrant colors the water at sunset offered. "No, the family prefers the beach house or the manor for gatherings. This is my place. My solitude."

"So, you just have parties here, then?" She closed her eyes in bliss as Michael Bublé began to croon throughout the dwelling.

"I will admit that my Team has gathered here for a few relaxing days. But it has been a 'men-only' excursion. You know...drinking beer, not having any manners, the whole male-bonding thing."

"Having seen your Team, I would hate to be the one to clean up after that! I bet you are one rowdy bunch!" She laughed as her eyes opened in time to witness the final fading of the colors from the setting of the sun.

His body swayed against hers in time with the music. "Dance with me," he purred in her ear.

Without a single protest, Alexis spun around in his arms and let his body lead hers slowly but with incredible grace around the open space in front of the windows. Her eyes closed again and she rested her head against his chest.

"You feel so perfect here in my arms, Lex. So perfect," he murmured as darkness fell over the land, immersing the dancers.

Oh, you speak the truth, Scott. I love being in your arms. She couldn't say anything out loud; her entire body was enjoying the feel of being in his solid embrace. If only they could dance forever.

"We should get changed if we are going to get something to eat," he said as the music picked up its beat.

"What type of place are we going to? A jean-and-tee place or something that requires me to dress up?"

His eyes seemed to burn as he gazed upon her. "Jeans. I thought we would eat and then go shopping so we don't have to go into town tomorrow unless we wanted to."

"Cool." She removed herself from his touch and asked, "Can you turn on some lights so I don't kill myself here?"

"Don't move. I'll get some on." Moments later the room was enveloped in a soft light from the recessed and track lighting.

"This place is absolutely amazing," she said, maneuvering around the leather furniture to reach the stairs. She was oblivious to the stare that was fixed like epoxy to her hind end.

※

The new couple walked into the restaurant easily. Alexis nodded as she glanced around. It smelled heavenly in here and the place looked clean. It was just a small out-of-the-way joint that seemed to serve hearty food, the kind she loved to eat. There wasn't one aroma in particular that tempted her nose; it was the combination of the fries, steaks, and everything else the place offered.

"Smells great," she said with a smile.

"They have good food," Scott spoke as his hand settled on the small of her back.

"Scott!" a feminine voice yelled from inside the dining area. Seconds later, a petite, buxom blonde came up, jumped into his arms, and tried to kiss him.

The woman was unsuccessful. "Lucy, stop it." He set her down and moved closer to Alexis.

The blonde pouted, sticking out her lower lip. A lip, in Alexis's mind, that had been given a shot to make it look fatter. This woman seemed to barely have an original part on her anywhere. Still, she was very attractive, and that made Alexis feel uneasy. "Why didn't you tell me you were back, Scott?" Lucy said in that annoying little-girl whine.

"I just got back. I'd like to introduce you to my date. Lucy Reingold, meet Alexis Rogets." His hand slid to rest on Alexis's back once again, an act that Miss Reingold noticed.

Baby blues narrowed as she plastered a false grin on her face. "Nice to meet you, Alexis. Where do you know my Scott from? What do you do? I am going to be a medical assistant. Scott likes professional women. He is in the Navy...a SEAL." Lucy imparted with an assumed wisdom, like she was all-important to know it.

"Oh, no, the pleasure is all mine. I love meeting his friends." Alexis was being polite, almost professional.

"Well, like I said, he loves professional women, which is why *I* am going to be one."

I bet you already are one, just not the kind you want advertised, you freakin' little 'ho. "Well, I wish you all the best with that." She smiled gently before her cat-eyed gaze turned to Scott and sent him a message saying she wanted to move on.

"It was good seeing you again, Lucy. I'm afraid you'll have to excuse us, we are about to get something to eat." He tried to move past but she stepped in front of Alexis, glowering at her.

"Don't think you have any hold over him. He doesn't need a woman on welfare to take care of. I know you want him for his money. I've known him for a long time." Her eyes were narrowed even further and her voice came out in one long hiss. "Do you even have a job?"

"Not really," Alexis ground out. Her eyes began to glow with an eerie spark that made Lucy take a slight step back. "I mean, since I graduated from Harvard with my measly little M.D., I just play in the Navy. I don't really do much work." Those angry eyes cut over to slice into the man beside her.

"Please excuse us, Lucy, my date and I want to get some dinner and our table is ready." Less politely this time, he brushed past the rude woman and escorted a still-rigid Alexis to their table. "Sorry about that," he whispered in her ear as she sat down and he slid her chair in at the table.

Alexis just shrugged. *Two choices here, Lex. One, be mad and ruin the whole evening; or two, accept that he is an extremely handsome man and many women are going to know him, especially if his family has a home here — not to mention the cabin in which you and he are sharing a room tonight, so buck up. He is taking you home with him.* "You don't have to apologize to me," she said in a relatively calm voice.

Looking across the table, Scott waited to see if the tension would leave her body. He groaned as he didn't notice any of it dissipate. *Figures that damn Lucy would ruin what could very well have been the best night of my life.* "I didn't want to make you uncomfortable and Lucy has a way of doing that."

One side of her mouth turned up in a sarcastic smile. "Trust me, it would take much more than whatever that little wannabe has to offer to make me uncomfortable. I shouldn't have gotten snippy with her so I apologize."

A blond eyebrow rose. "Why would you apologize? I think it's wonderful you were jealous of her."

Her eyes narrowed slightly. "I was *not* jealous. And I was apologizing because I am sure you know lots of people around here and I don't want to be the cause of any discontent between you and them."

Scott winked at her. "You *were* jealous." He fell silent as the waiter came and took their order. After the man left, he sent her another knee-knocking grin. "I find that sexy as hell."

"You are incorrigible. Do you know that?" Alexis asked after watching him for a while.

He flashed a brilliant white smile. "So I have been told from time to time." She shook her head in mock irritation but held her tongue because their food had arrived.

It was dark as he pulled the black Corvette into the almost-empty parking lot of the grocery store. Scott waited for her and walked beside her into the store, his callused hand once again settled at the base of her spine. He grabbed the cart and said, "See, I told you I knew how to shop."

"All I see is a man who is holding onto a shopping cart. That isn't shopping. I will be impressed once I see how you shop and what you buy." Alexis crossed her arms and sent him a skeptical look.

"Oh, I am all good, baby, all good," he said in that seductive purr he had and leaned in closer, "and I am so looking forward to showing you just how good I am."

Biting the inside of her lip to keep from smiling or showing him how his words affected her, Alexis lifted one shoulder and dropped it nonchalantly. "Big talk from a man. What a surprise. I am still waiting to be impressed." Her tiger eyes were full of humor as she watched for his reaction.

She didn't have long to wait. His strong arms reached out and swept her into his embrace. Putting them nose to nose, he growled, "Don't test me, woman, I will leave this store in a second and take you home."

Her tongue snuck out and licked along the corner of his mouth. "Well, now, that may impress me."

Scott shuddered. "I should have called ahead and had the house stocked with food, that way I could take you home right now. But we need some food, 'cause I know we will be working up an appetite." His tongue repaid the favor by teasing her lips.

"Well, I like caramel and chocolate sauce. A little whipped cream is also nice." Her eyes flashed with barely restrained passion.

A groan slipped out of his mouth seconds before he descended upon her full, begging-to-be-kissed mouth. Dragging his lips off hers, he mumbled, "You are a wicked and naughty woman. Let's get going so we can get the hell out of here." Another fast kiss and he was practically dragging her through the store, tossing items into the cart.

※

The drive back to the cabin was quicker than it should have been had he been obeying all traffic laws. Scott's mind was full of images of the woman beside him without clothes on. He wanted her so badly, his body hurt.

Turning into the driveway he swore, "Damn it all to hell!"

Alexis glanced from him to the house. "What is it?"

"My brother is here," he said in a resigned tone.

"How can you tell?"

"I left the light on low; now it's on medium." He turned off the car and tightened his hands around the steering wheel. *Why in the hell am I only allowed to get so close to her before something or someone intrudes?*

"You haven't mentioned your brothers all that much, and while I know you have two brothers and one sister, do you not get along?"

"We have our moments. But I didn't want to do anything except take you in the house and make love to you."

Her soft eyes met his in the soft ceiling light of the car. "We have a week together. I want to make love to you, too, but we can't stay out here in the car. There are perishable items in here and I need to check your wound again."

She wants to make love. Scott felt his body twitch in response. "Okay." He got out of the car and opened the door for her. They each gathered a few bags from the trunk and headed to the door. Scott unlocked it and kicked it open with a foot, yelling as soon as he got in the cabin, "Reeve? Where are you?"

"Don't yell, Scott. I'm right here," a deep voice reached them as a man walked into view.

He was tall, maybe two inches shorter than Scott, and in good shape, though not even close to his brother's league as it was difficult for most people to be in the same physical shape as a Navy SEAL. His facial features were similar to Scott's as well, though he was dark-haired where Scott was light.

"What are you doing here?" Scott asked as he stepped aside for Alexis to slide up next to him, carrying her handful of bags.

Reeve didn't answer; his dark eyes had landed upon the curvaceous black woman who stood next to the eldest Leighton brother while holding about five bags of groceries. "Who are you?" he questioned.

"My name is Lex," she said as she skirted around the man in her way and walked towards the kitchen.

"Reeve, there are six more bags in the car. Get them and bring 'em to the kitchen," Scott ordered as he moved into the kitchen, fully expecting his brother to do as he was told. He did.

When the black-haired man walked into the kitchen with the remaining bags in his hands, the light music of a cell phone went off. Alexis reached for her phone, flipping it open. "Rogets." With a wave to Scott, whose eyes had narrowed, she headed out of the kitchen to take her call in private, allowing the brothers a chance to talk.

Chapter Ten

"What is going on here, Scott?" Reeve asked, though Scott didn't let up his possessive observance of the woman leaving the room with her phone cradled to her ear.

"I am on vacation. What are you doing here?" He didn't even glance at Reeve, waiting for Alexis to come back into the kitchen.

"I was at the beach house and saw you come in for the keys to your cabin. Why didn't you tell us you were home? We've been worried about you." The second oldest, Reeve got along the best with Scott.

"I haven't been home that long."

"Long enough to get a woman. Where'd you pick her up? Granted she is a good looking piece of—"

"Brother or not, if you value your life that sentence will never be finished." Scott issued the warning in a deadly calm voice.

Reeve shivered at the look in his brother's eyes. "Who is she, Scott?"

"Her name is Alexis Rogets. And before your mind even begins to think like that, she isn't after my money. She is a doctor."

One dark eyebrow arched as Reeve cocked his head. "Is this the one from two years ago that had you off women?" That deep voice turned teasing.

Scott wanted to snap at his brother for putting it like that, but if he were willing to tease him about his attraction to Lex then all the better, for it was preferable to the alternative. His family, being from old Southern money, could have views that made Scott's skin crawl at times. "She's the one."

"A doctor?" Reeve winked. "Well, considering what you do for a living, I guess you should have one around."

"Very funny, little brother. Keep that up and you will be glad she is around to fix you up after I kick the crap out of you," Scott snapped playfully.

"Hey, I'm only speaking the truth." Reeve sobered up for a second. "Aren't you breaking some sort of protocol being with her?"

"No!" His hands clenched as he bit off his response. "We aren't in the same command, so we aren't breaking any rules."

"Works for me. So, tell me, what does she see in an ugly mug like yours? You know she is gonna want someone handsome."

"Just keep on shoveling the shit, Charleston Reeve Kirkland Leighton, just keep on shovelin'," Scott dared him.

"Man, don't call me that. You know I hate my name."

"Truce?" Scott offered.

"Okay. I need to talk to you anyway."

With another glance that afforded him a view of Alexis walking back and forth in front of the large windows in the front room, he once again turned his attention to his brother. "About what?"

Reeve also looked to make sure Alexis was preoccupied. Content that she was, he answered his older sibling. "About Marisol."

The eldest Leighton brother froze at that name. Marisol Anderson was this area's "bad girl." Sure she was easy on the eyes, but she could be the poster girl for the slogan, "Beauty is only skin deep." If anyone thought of any horrible word and were to look it up in the dictionary, they would find a picture of Marisol right next to it.

Spite and a healthy dose of vindictiveness continually coursed through her veins. For a long while, her sights had been set on one Harrington Prescott Broderick Leighton, III, wanting desperately to land a piece of the fortune that would be passed onto him.

Fortunately for Scott, he'd been dating a girl at the time and that allowed him to see Marisol for who she really was. Evil. A doppelganger. Apparently, his warnings had gone unheeded by his brother. Praying for the ability to be objective and not rant or rave, Scott calmly asked, "What about Marisol?"

Reeve allowed himself another furtive glance ensuring the privacy of their conversation. "She called me today, which was who I was on the phone with when you stopped by the beach house. Anyway, she said she's pregnant." He paused for a second before adding the words that Scott didn't want to hear. "It's mine."

Jesus. "Ahh, Reeve, what have you done?" Scott asked, setting his large frame down on a stool.

Anger flashed in those dark eyes. "She loves me, man. She told me so. I was hoping you'd understand, but..." He shrugged.

"How do you know it's yours and she's not just playing you?" Scott argued.

Reeve slammed his hand down on the counter. "I could ask you the same thing, bringing *her* into the family." His words were hissed.

"Be very careful with the next words out of your mouth, Reeve." Scott's whole body had become tense and battle-ready.

"At least the woman I got pregnant is white and will be accepted into the family fold." Reeve hurled carelessly.

In less time than it took Reeve to blink, Scott had tossed him up against the wall, momentarily stunning him. One large hand began to close off the windpipe of the younger kinsman. "That woman who claims you got her pregnant is a liar and a whore," Scott ground out between clenched teeth. "The only thing y'all probably shared is some STD." He lowered his face to his younger brother's.

"Don't you ever, *ever*, think about implying something racial like this again. Especially not about Lex. She is more of a woman than Marisol will ever be. She got her M.D. from Harvard and is the best damn doctor I know." The hand closed tighter. "If you feel the need to keep those particular views on race, then do so without me in your life." Scott stepped away from his brother as if he no longer could stand to touch him.

Gasping for air, Reeve rubbed his sore throat. Scott had never done anything like that to him before, but he'd never been so angry, either. He picked up the stool he'd knocked over and sat back down on it.

Growing up, Scott would never let him or Godric, the youngest brother, speak ill of another person because of the color of their skin. But it seemed after he left for the Navy, Reeve had fallen into more of the mindset of his family, which was an act that placed him in total opposition to Scott's beliefs.

Reeve held his hands out in silent plea. "I'm sorry, man. I always say things I don't mean when I get defensive." No expression moved across Scott's face. "I know she wanted you. Marisol, man...I'm talking about Marisol."

With a cautious step, Reeve approached the bar well aware Scott regarded him with expressionless eyes. "She offered to leave if I paid her. She said although she loves me, she didn't want Mom and Dad to disown me."

"Of course not," Scott stated. "If you get cut off then there will be no more money for her."

"I really screwed up, didn't I?" Reeve muttered.

"You're not a baby anymore, Reeve. You need to grow up and act like an adult. You're thirty-four. You are more than capable of making something of yourself instead of living off the allowance that Mom and Dad give you."

"I'll never measure up to your expectations, will I, Scott?"

"You don't have to prove anything to me. It's your life, not mine." There was not a single thread of sympathy in Scott's voice.

The SEAL's entire being softened his blue eyes saw Alexis in the doorway. "Done with your call?" Scott asked, as one arm reached out and beckoned her over to him.

Alexis nodded as she flowed in her easy gait towards his muscled body. "I didn't want to interrupt your conversation, but the food needs to be put away." Her dark hand reached out and caressed the side of his cheek before dropping back to her side.

His arm slid around her waist. "Who called you?" Scott couldn't stop the question even if he wanted to, shocking himself a little; out of all the women he'd been with, there had been none he'd acted possessive about. Until now.

A radiant smile lit her dark loveliness. "Kieran. He wanted to know where I was."

Scott tried to pretend he was fine with that response, but ten seconds later he prompted, "And?"

Alexis touched her finger to the end of his Romanesque nose and grinned impishly. "I said I was on vacation with a man and we were staying at his cabin by the beach. Kieran wanted to know where and I said I was fine, wasn't gonna tell him, and that you would keep me perfectly safe."

So long as there is breath in my body, I will keep you safe, healer of my heart. "Of course I will keep you safe." He actually sounded offended.

"I know." She stepped away from his lingering touch and began to put things away.

Scott met briefly the now-amused gaze of his brother briefly before watching Alexis move comfortably around his kitchen. "Lex," he uttered.

"Yes?" Without turning around, she continued to put things away.

"Were you planning on telling me who Kieran is?" His fingers began to drum along the top of the bar where he was sitting.

"Hadn't planned on it, no." She closed the fridge door and began to empty another bag.

The blond man got off his stool and stalked her. "Plan on it," he said on a low rumble.

"Kieran is my third-oldest brother." Alexis squealed as he picked her up and turned her toward him.

"Naughty little healer."

She smiled and giggled. "You were jealous."

"Always." He brought her closer for a kiss.

Still holding Alexis, Scott turned and found that his brother stood watching them with a mixture of clarity and longing on his face. Maybe their previous conversation was getting though to him "Will you be all right, Reeve?" he asked as he sat his lovely healer on a stool and stood behind her, allowing their bodies to remain in constant contact.

"I guess I don't really have a choice," Reeve sighed and occupied a seat across from Alexis. He rested his dark gaze upon her more golden one.

"I can leave if you all would like to talk in private," she offered, correctly reading the hesitation in Reeve's eyes. Alexis didn't wait for a response before sliding off the barstool and walking out of the kitchen. "It was nice to meet you, Reeve Leighton," she commented over her shoulder.

※

Walking down the path to the beach, Alexis was at peace. The solar-charged lanterns with the soft amber covers illuminated her way with their gentle glow. Her sandals were silent as she ambled over the asphalt that made up the path.

The tranquil ocean breeze wrapped itself around her like a lover's caress. As she left the path and began to traipse across the sand, her eyes landed on the sliver of the moon that was beginning to rise over the ocean. Her serene gaze lingered on it before scanning the endless sky, watching as star after star became visible.

This was the life. Alexis glided along the water's edge, taking off her sandals and dangling them from her fingers. The surf lapped at her toes and took away any tension left in her body. She walked until the moon had risen above the horizon.

Turning around, her contented body took her back to where she knew she'd entered the beach. As she was walking along, Alexis made out a figure strolling towards her. Instinctively, her body tensed before her brain processed that walk. Scott. Her body began to tremble for a different reason and her insides got all fluttery.

"Are you okay?" were the first words out of his mouth as his arms drew her into his chest.

She inhaled deeply, her body taking in the masculine smells that made up Scott. "Of course. Why?"

"You've been gone well over an hour."

That long? "Wow. I guess time just slipped away from me. I was just enjoying the night."

Scott moved to her side and picked up her free hand to intertwine their fingers. "Was. Did you want to be alone?"

How in the hell am I supposed to think straight with him touching me? "No, don't leave. Stay with me." Her hand tightened around his.

"Your wish is my command," he responded in a voice that was purely sexual.

"Where is your brother?" She tried to take deep breaths and slow her rapidly beating heart.

"He went home. He has some serious thinking to do."

"I don't want to be the cause of problems between you and your family," she said as they headed back up the beach.

"Don't worry about them. This is our time," he purred into her ear.

"Thank you. Thank you for sharing this place with me. It is so beautiful here." Her words were full of wonder as she gestured around her with her other hand. "This is what I love about being in the Navy. Standing on deck at night, looking out at all of this…this beauty."

"I am the one who should be thanking you, for coming with me. For trusting in me enough to come here." Scott stopped walking and faced them out to sea and put her body against the front of his. "Do you want to go swimming?"

"I don't have a swimsuit on."

"Don't tell me you have never gone skinny-dipping." His breath teased her ear.

"Not in a very long time, and never with a man."

Never with another man, if I have my way. And I usually do. "Well, there is a first time for everything. Come on," he coaxed. "Let's go swimming."

"Is it safe?" Her whole body shivered at the thought of going in the water with him totally naked.

"I'd keep you safe." His lips nibbled on her earlobe.

"So, that's a no. Besides, with your gunshot wound I don't think you should be in the water."

He chuckled. "When in doubt, fall back on being a doctor. Okay, let's go back to the house, and you can check my wound."

"I am getting kind of tired."

"It has been a long day."

But something about the look in Scott's eyes told Alexis it wasn't over yet.

Chapter Eleven

It was after midnight when they shut the front door behind them and were once again in his beautiful cabin. They had walked slowly along the beach, holding hands and stargazing.

Scott made short work of locking up his house before he took her hand and led her though the entrance to the large lighted kitchen, where he whipped off his shirt easily to stand bare-chested before her. Masculine arrogance filled his gaze as he watched Alexis stand there and practically drool over his hard body before she remembered what she was supposed to be doing.

"Raise your arm," she ordered. "How does it feel? Any pain? Tenderness?" The doctor rattled off questions until she was content that he was mending well. Checking the condition of the stitches, she looked up from her kneeling position at the man watching her. "You heal at an amazing rate. A wound like this would disable most men."

He gave a careless shoulder lift. "I have had worse." Scott wasn't bragging, just stating the cold, hard facts.

"That is what scares me," she whispered, not realizing he heard her.

"Come here, Alexis," he said softly as he lifted her and placed her on the breakfast bar positioning himself between her legs. "Look at me," he ordered in that same hushed voice. "Is that why you keep trying to avoid your feelings for me? Because of what I do, who I am?" His fingers gripped her chin and forced her to look at him.

"I'm sure that's part of it," she admitted.

"And the others would be the difference in our ranks and the whole color thing, right?" He never released her gaze, just stared into her soul with those piercing blue eyes of his.

"Those are two points as well," Alexis conceded.

"There is something more?" His eyes narrowed.

"Yes." Her response was fast and direct.

"And what would that be?"

"The fact that my feelings for you scare the hell out of me. I feel so out of control around you, saying things, doing things that I wouldn't be doing normally." Her fingers traced his collarbone and outlined his ear. He shivered beneath the tips of her digits.

"And tonight?" His question was quiet in the room but it echoed throughout her soul like a bass drum.

Alexis pressed her full lips to his and gave him her answer that way. Each stroke of her tongue against his told him she wanted him, in no uncertain terms. As she sucked on his lower lip, he groaned. Her legs drew him in closer to the apex of her thighs and she was the one who released a moan as she felt his erection press against her. "Please," she whimpered. "Please, Scott."

The last syllable hadn't even faded from the air before he swept her up into his arms as he took the stairs two at a time. *This is the first time she willingly called me Scott without having to be told.* His heart pounded so hard with the anticipation of enjoying the woman of his dreams.

His barefoot slammed his bedroom door shut behind him as he lay her down on the bed to turn on a bedside light. "I have waited for this night for so long," he murmured as his mouth latched back onto hers.

"As have I." she whispered.

Standing up straight without relinquishing his hold on her, Scott set her on her feet. His strong hands slid up her hips and latched onto the hem of her shirt. With a slow deliberate motion he pulled it up, exposing her rich, toffee-colored torso to his gaze. Throwing the shirt off to the side, he looked at the spectacular woman before him. Her eyes were on his face, watching every emotion he showed.

He took his time enjoying the view. Her bra was lacy, sea-foam green in color, and barely seemed to contain her full breasts. Swallowing hard, his eyes continued their downward perusal. Her belly was flat, toned and yet—to his pleasure—distinctly feminine.

Scott undid the button on her capris and then unzipped them. As the khaki material slid down over the flare of her hips, a pair of bikini-style panties in the same color as the bra met his gaze. Kneeling before her, he lifted one silken leg and then the other, freeing her from the pants.

"You are amazing," came his guttural groan as he stood once again.

Alexis reached for the waistband of his jeans and undid the button. Her eyes were focused on the mid-region of his body, lustfully and without an ounce of shame. That moist tongue of hers snuck out and wet her lips before her fingers moved again.

Carefully, she lowered the zipper and tugged his form-fitting jeans off lean hips and down his hairy legs. She, too, dropped to her knees and removed the pants completely, leaving him in nothing but a pair of navy blue boxers that did little to contain the hard ridge within them.

Her hands ran up his legs from his ankles to his hips. Alexis stood as her hands moved up his body. From his hips she trailed her fingers up the washboard stomach, across the marbled pectorals, up to his shoulders and across the back of his shorn head. Lacing her fingers there, she nudged him towards her and her waiting mouth.

Eventually, the couple made it to Scott's bedroom. Once there, two mouths met with heated passion as their owners stood pressed against one another wearing only their underclothing. Sparks flew between heated flesh as tongues once again dueled for supremacy. Scott won.

It was with skill that he wrested control of the kiss away from the woman who had taken a part of his soul into her body. Once again in control, Scott changed the tempo of the kiss. He backed off and the exchange grew softer. Still keeping his lips pressed against hers, he walked them back towards the bed and lay them down on his firm mattress.

"You still have more clothes on than I do," he whispered against her swollen lips.

"More articles perhaps, but not material," she teased as her hands traced small patterns on the back of his head.

"Too many." Scott's hands skillfully removed her bra replacing the material with his callused hands. His thumbs ran over her already tight nipples, making them tighten even more.

Alexis arched her back, pressing herself more fully into his touch. "*Yesss*," she hissed as her hand moved down the front of his boxer shorts. She groaned, a sound echoed by the man in bed with her, as she closed her hand around his throbbing erection.

"Jesus, Lex." His hips bucked against her hand.

"Scott." That word was a mixture of a command and a plea. It screamed of things she couldn't find the words to say, but desperately craved.

One of his hands left her breast and slipped beneath the elastic on her panties and with one fast jerk broke it. As her body was trying to recover from the force of that tug he slipped one long finger inside her wet body.

Her scream was muted by lack of air. Exotic eyes rolled back into her head as she felt her body close around his finger. "You feel so good, Lex," he purred into her ear at the same time his other hand tweaked her taut nipple, causing another whole shudder to go through her. A shudder that he felt with the finger buried deep within her.

The palm of his hand pressed against her clit and with each motion it sent wave after wave of pleasure through her body. Clamping her thighs around his wrist, Alexis kept him where she wanted. He added another finger to her and when he did, a scream managed to escape. "Scott!"

"I'm right here, my love. Right here," he muttered. Scott tried to control himself, but her hand around his manhood did little to help him out. As her body convulsed around his fingers, he knew he couldn't wait any longer.

His boxers disappeared and he settled his large body between her widespread thighs. Fingers coated with her desire moved from her thighs to his mouth and he sucked them clean, never allowing her gaze to drop from his. "I want you, Lex."

One of her hands clutched his side as the other one, instead of grabbing his wound, wrapped around his large penis and ran a finger over the large, wet head of it. "Please, Scott, don't make me wait any longer."

He groaned at her words. As he removed her hand and placed himself at the opening of her womanhood, he hesitated. *Don't be an animal, Scott.*

She whimpered and lifted her hips in invitation. "Scott," she pled.

"What about protection?" He wasn't wearing condom.

"I'm on the Pill," she ground out as her legs slid around his waist encouraging him to enter.

That was all he needed to hear. With one fast stroke he was completely sheathed inside her velvet warmth. At her sharp intake of breath, he stopped to allow them both to get used to the feeling. He was in heaven; she felt so good around him.

Alexis's eyes rolled back. It felt like every part of her body stretched to accommodate his thick length.

As her eyes fluttered open to meet his tender gaze, Scott began to move within her. His hips delivered his thick erection slowly in and out of her, steady strokes that left them both wanting something more.

The pace was erotically slow. He slid almost all the way out of her body, then met her eyes and held them as his length slipped all the way back in until he was absolutely encased by her heat.

"Scott," her tormented whisper reached him.

"Yes, my love, what is it?" In and out he stroked as beads of sweat formed on his head from trying not to lose control.

Her body was so close to finding the release she so desperately wanted to claim. "Please," she begged.

Bracing his hands on either side of her head, he sucked in her earlobe and began to increase the speed and intensity of each stroke he delivered. Latching her legs around his waist, Alexis's hands had formed claws and were digging into his shoulder blades.

Scott plunged harder, faster, and deeper. Her pants changed to moans and then into screams as he pounded into her willing body. "Come for me," he ordered as his hips drilled his thick cock deep into her.

She did. Her back arched as her hips met his thrust sending him deeper yet. As her internal muscles clamped down around him Scott couldn't hold himself back and with one last plunge he came inside her as he shouted his release to the cabin.

Limbs shaking, he collapsed next to her. Their bodies were covered with sweat and eagerly absorbed the cool air that was coming in from the open bedroom window. Scott tucked her into his body before his eyes closed and he just enjoyed the feeling of completion, oneness, contentment, and fulfillment. "Are you okay?" The heavy timbre of his voice broke the silence.

"Fine, just fine." She snuggled up closer to his amazing body. "And you?"

"I feel like I just ran about ten clicks with a full pack on, but good other than that."

Rolling one eye towards him, Alexis grumbled. "Well, if being in bed with me can be likened to one of your workouts, maybe I should just leave." She made like she was getting up only to find his embrace had turned to steel.

"My heart is just pounding that hard. Trust me, I would rather have this kind of workout any day." His lips spoke against her head. "I mean that as a compliment."

"Some compliment."

"What you would rather I tell you? That I have never felt like this before with anyone?" His fingers teased the skin on her arms.

She shrugged, trying to act unaffected. "Only tell me the truth."

His tone grew serious. "Alexis, I have never felt like this before with anyone. My heart feels like it is about to poke a hole in my chest, it is pounding so hard. I am having a hard time breathing and at the same time, I feel like all is right with the world." One hand moved her face to meet his. "I am holding the woman I have been dreaming about for the past two years in my arms, and I am experiencing a feeling I have never felt before."

Her eyes narrowed briefly before he continued. "I want this forever. I want you to be in my life from now until the day we die. I have never been in love before so I am new at this feeling—regardless of that, I know I love you. I love you, Lex." His eyes echoed the sincerity of his words.

Tiger eyes widened but she remained silent as his hand settled over her mouth. "Let me finish. I know you will try to pass this off as me being in the moment. It's not. I love you, Alexis. I am praying that your Pill won't work and this night, *our night* of lovemaking, will result in a child." He shook his head. "Please, don't say anything. I have something else in mind." Scott replaced his hand over her mouth with his lips.

A few hours later, the lovers were sound asleep on the messy bed, sheets torn from the mattress and the comforter was on the floor somewhere. Both bodies were devoid of clothing and even as they lay in silent slumber, his large hand rested possessively on her belly. Or was it resting there in hopes that a future generation had defied her precaution and taken root?

※

Her legs were burning but Alexis kept pounding away. She inhaled each and every painful breath gratefully. Her ponytail bounced with each stride she took as her legs pumped up and down, taking her along the beach. *He said he loved you, girl! What are you doing out here? You should be in bed with him!*

"I don't know what makes him think he loves me," she panted as she jogged on. *Can't run forever, girl.* "The hell I can't. I should be going back; maybe it was a sleep deprivation thing." *You know that ain't even true. He told you he loved you!*

"Maybe it was a slip of the tongue." She turned around to head back up the beach when her mind jumped back in the conversation. *You know what his tongue is like, and that was no slip.* "He doesn't know me well enough," she argued with herself. *Seems to me that last night he got to know the bit of you he hadn't known yet.*

She tried ignoring the running inner-commentary her brain was inopportunely providing, focusing on her jog while talking herself through last night and her feelings. "If I pay no heed to what he said, perhaps he won't mention it either." *You know hearing those words from him was like being handed the moon.* "Men always say things they don't mean when they are in bed having sex." *Sex? You didn't have sex, y'all made love. Slow, tender, and sweet, sweet love.*

Body throbbing at the memories of how his touch inflamed her nerves, Alexis stumbled and took a minute to regain her surefooted strides. "It was sex! Granted, really, *really* good sex but sex just the same." Her mouth clamped shut as she realized she had blurted that out while jogging past an old couple walking. She could feel eyes watching her retreating back. *Please, you know that couple is still gettin' they swerve on!*

Alexis slowed to a walk as she rolled her eyes and began her cool-down process. There were times her brain was like a whole other entity within her. *There are medical terms for that. Dissociation. Schizophrenia.* Rubbing her temples, her body instinctively fell into her usual pace as she tried to shut out her brain's ramblings.

Twenty minutes later, her cooled-down body stood at the edge of the asphalt path. Her body was sore, both from her run and spending the night with a man named Scott. Point blank, she was tired. But it was a good tired. Very good.

As she was reforming her disastrous ponytail, a large set of masculine hands reached around her. "Why didn't you wait for me? I would've run with you."

I needed to think on some things. "I don't think I could keep up with you."

His teeth nipped at her neck. "You did fine last night." His tongue gently caressed the spot where he had bitten, as if to heal it. "How are you feeling this morning?"

"Good," she answered, leaning her sweaty body against his dry one.

"Well, good. Make yourself at home, Alexis. I am going to take a short run." His hands caressed her belly as if he imagined her carrying his child already. "I love you," Scott whispered before slipping past her and moving off down the beach, looking dangerous and graceful at the same time. Like a shark. How fitting.

Alexis walked into his cabin and took in the splendor it offered again. "Damn, this is a nice place." The phone rang but she ignored it as she walked up the polished stairs to the master bedroom. Grabbing another set of clothes, she entered the marbled bathroom where she stood contentedly under the pounding spray of three water heads that massaged away her soreness.

Twenty minutes later she was back downstairs, her body dry, lotioned, and dressed, standing in the kitchen and pouring herself a glass of orange juice. Taking the glass she went out to the porch that wrapped around the home. Choosing one of the built-in benches, she sat down on the cushion and watched as the sun climbed higher in the sky over the ocean.

Chapter Twelve

Holding a plate of fresh fruit in his hands, Scott stopped outside the sliding glass door and just stared. There Alexis sat, her back against the railing, as her golden-brown gaze overlooked the ocean. Propped beside her on the rail was an empty glass.

Her legs were drawn up to her chest, hands locked around the shins, and her chin rested on her knees. She wore a plum tee-shirt and a pair of gray sweats, her bare feet stuck out from beneath the soft material. Hair that shone in the morning sun hung free around her.

Finally, she is in my place. And now that I have experienced my life with her in it, I don't want to experience it without her. His eyes drifted to her abdomen and he sighed. *Please let there be a child growing in her.*

Padding across the smooth cedar deck, he moved his freshly showered body towards the woman who ignored him. Her gaze never left the water.

Sliding the full plate beneath her nose, he interrupted her silent musings. "Fruit?"

Her body jerked. "Oh, I didn't hear you," she said in her throaty voice. "When did you get back?" She glanced at her watch. "What time is it?"

"I haven't been back long." He smiled as Alexis took the plate from him and crossed her legs so he could sit in front of her.

Her gaze flicked over him. "Long enough to shower and shave."

"I was sweaty." Eyes darkened with memories of being sweaty with her.

Popping a fat blueberry in her mouth, she swallowed it before she smiled. "So, what is on the agenda for today?"

His eyes drifted over her body with obvious desire. "You are in charge, Alexis, my love. You tell me what you want to do."

Alexis shuddered at the sexual innuendo in his rich voice. Her eyes took in the fact that all he wore was a pair of faded blue jeans that adhered to his body like nobody's business. Her eyes grew hooded as she ate a few more succulent blueberries. "What around here is good?"

"I am." Scott leaned over the plate that sat between them and kissed her. She tasted of blueberries and Alexis.

With a moan, she opened her mouth to accept his searching tongue. One of her legs dropped to the floor as her body pressed towards his.

Scott drew back, his eyes riveted on her with a promise in them. He picked up a bite-sized chunk of honeydew and slipped the juicy fruit between her lips. His tongue swept away the remains of the juice on her chin. "Would you like to go scuba diving?" he asked, observing her as she enjoyed the fruit.

After she swallowed, Alexis took a wedge of kiwi and held it out for him. As his mouth drew in her fingers along with the green treat, he saw her eyes flash. "Yes," she purred. "Scuba diving would be wonderful."

"Let's get going or we won't be going at all. Well, we'd be going somewhere but not anywhere close to the boat." Scott popped a few more bites of fruit in his mouth as he stood and waited for Alexis to go ahead of him.

※

"I am going to have to put a waterproof sealant on that wound of yours," Alexis announced as he drove them to the marina.

"You do care. You don't want me to be hurt." He smiled, tossing a glance at her.

She smirked. "No, I don't want my shark wrangler to die on me and leave me as bait for those things."

Rich laughter filled the car. "So I'm just protection?"

"Pretty much." Alexis watched him out of the corner of her eye.

Scott scowled. "Maybe I should just pull over here along this stretch of highway and show you just how important I am. And what other uses I have to offer you."

Making out with you in a 'Vette? Bad thoughts. Horny thoughts. "My, aren't we touchy."

He growled. "I could be."

Alexis reached across the car and trailed her fingers along one rock hard thigh. "I hope you are. But later," she added as his eyes grew dark. Her soft laughter filled the car at his frustrated face.

"You are up on your cert, right?" he asked, the wind rushing over them in the top-down convertible.

"I'm good. Just redid it last month." She cut her intoxicating eyes to him and said, "I'm not even going to ask you."

Scott just smiled as he pulled into the marina and drove down to slip 4B. Turning off the car, he got out and opened Alexis's door for her. After shutting it, he leaned against the door only to tug her back into him, his strong thighs cradling her softer ones between them.

Lean fingers brushed her hair back from her neck in an affectionate gesture, exposing the string that held up her bikini top. Her eyes were curious as she spoke. "What's the matter?"

"Nothing," he admitted in that deep voice of his. "I just wanted to hold you." Fingertips danced along her arms.

"'Kay," Alexis responded as her body sank against his.

For a few moments they just stood together in each other's arms. "You do know that what I said to you last night was real, right?"

Her eyes flew open but she couldn't move because his arms seemed to solidify around her, becoming immovable. "Look—"

"No, you look, or rather listen since if I loosen my grip you will run. I meant each and every one of those words that I said to you. *Every single one—*"

"Harrier!" a loud shout interrupted him. "Hell, man, I was beginning to wonder if you were ever gonna show up!"

Alexis jumped but found herself still unable to get free. "Hey, Terry," Scott said as his hands continued to caress her skin. Turning her head, Alexis was surprised to see a large black man striding towards them. He was huge all over, nothing but muscle.

The newcomer's black eyes ran smoothly over the woman held in his friend's embrace. "Is this her? Makes sense that you would be late." The booming question came as the man slowed to a stop before Scott.

With a smile, Scott let go of Alexis and hugged the man named Terry. "God, it is so good to see you, man," he said.

Trunk-like arms returned the hearty hug as Alexis spun, leaned back against the door of the black convertible, and watched the two friends' reunion. "It has been a long time. Now let me look at you." He pulled back, exposing a strikingly white smile against his dark skin and then hugged his friend again. "Looks like being a SEAL has been good for you."

Scott laughed. "Too long, my friend. It has been too long and, yes, being a SEAL does agree with me." He stepped back.

He had turned halfway towards Alexis when a feminine squeal filled the air. "*Hhhaaarrrrriiieeerrrr!*" Three sets of eyes turned towards the shriek and they all saw a very shapely and beautiful younger black woman running up the pier. From five feet away she jumped straight at the blond man, who caught her easily and spun her around. Those long limbs of hers encircled his body as she hugged him tight. "I've missed you," her husky voice said.

Drawing back, Scott smiled at the woman he held so familiarly in his arms. "Wow, Stacey, you are growing up so fast." He kissed her cheek. "You are one beautiful woman." Alexis narrowed her tawny-colored eyes slightly.

Stacey wrinkled up her nose. "I'm grown."

Scott nodded. "I can definitely see that." It was with obvious care that he set her back down on her own two feet.

"Who is that?" A hint of an attitude crossed Stacey's face as she pointed at Alexis standing impassively.

A smile crossed Scott's face as he met Terry's gaze. "Y'all, I would like to introduce you to Alexis Rogets. *Dr.* Alexis Rogets." One tanned hand reached back and brought the woman who was now the center of attention to stand in front of him. Scott slid one arm around her waist. "Alexis, I would like you to meet Terry West and his daughter Stacey."

With a kind smile she held out one hand. "It is nice to meet you, Mr. West. And you, Ms. West."

That same booming laugh filled the air. "Polite to a fault, Ms. Rogets. What are you doing with this lubber, anyway?"

Alexis raised an eyebrow. "I have met him a few times and he invited me down for the week. Please call me Lex."

"Lex it is. Call me Terry or Skipper like everyone else. Come on, pretty lady, I have some questions for you. And I know everyone else is dying to meet the woman Harrier brought with him." As if they'd known each other forever, Terry took her arm and began to lead her down towards the pier to where a fifty foot yacht was moored. About seven other people wandered around, waiting for the late arrivals.

"Lex," a deep voice purred behind her.

She turned and saw Scott staring at her intensely, ignoring the young woman beside him. "Yes?"

He approached and held her gaze until he was close enough to touch her and his lips descended upon hers. The kiss was quick, powerful, and proprietary. Everyone now knew that she was Harrier's woman. "I love you," he mouthed as he stepped back and allowed her to be acquired once again by his friend.

Limbs shaky, Alexis walked with the large man onto the waiting yacht, followed by Scott and Stacey who was busy sending glares at her back. Everyone there waited eagerly to meet her and, as blue eyes that could stop her heart watched over her, Alexis met everyone on board. They were all friends from the Officer Candidate School in Annapolis, Maryland. Terry had been Scott's roommate, so their friendship was the oldest. Stacey's mother had gone to the store one day and just never came back, so Terry had become a single father while still in high school and Stacey had known Scott for much of her life.

There were also two other couples. Brian and Randi Eddington had been married for about seven years now and spent much of the cruise saying how they were the palest thing out on the water with the exception of the yacht. Brian had been discharged for an injury the previous year but still carried himself like a proud military man. His wife was a child development psychologist.

The second couple was Devón and Jakobie Grant. Devón, an African-American, had met his wife during a Temporary Assigned Duty, TAD, in her native Germany. He was currently out of the service, choosing instead to be a civilian contractor and his wife was the stay-at-home mother of their four children.

The rest were single men, all of them pilots, all of them the potential next poster boy for the Navy…or any branch of the armed services, for that matter. There was Mario Archer, a stocky man who had a great smile; Antwon Hulton, who had rich, chocolate eyes and a dimple in his right cheek; and finally Tag Walker, the biggest flirt of them all. His green eyes were constantly full of mischief and he'd gotten himself tossed overboard more than once after they'd dropped anchor where they were eventually going to dive.

※

Laughing with the two women beside her, Alexis made her way back aft. She had finally removed her shirt and pants, leaving her clad in her Wedgewood-blue bikini and pale, creamy-white magnolia sarong that barely covered her firm ass. And all the men were drooling over her. Oblivious to the attention, she walked with the women and stood at the railing drinking a beer, totally enjoying the day.

Scott's eyes narrowed, especially after he noticed how much the three pilots were enjoying her body. He felt a stirring in his loins as he moved towards her, wearing nothing except his swim trunks. "Ladies," he said, slipping an arm around Lex.

They nodded at him and smiled as his large body blocked the view of the other men. The other women left them alone. "Hey," Alexis said with a smile. "This is wonderful, thank you."

One finger tipped her chin up so he could kiss her. She tasted like Lex and beer and the combination was amazing. "You are absolutely stunning," he whispered into her ear. "What are you trying to do to me? Kill me?" His tongue licked along her ear. "Or are you just wanting to make me jealous? It is killing me that they are staring at you."

"They're your friends. I doubt they are staring at me," she said with a shake of her head.

"Oh, trust me, they are staring. Especially Tag. I think you bewitched him," he grumbled, taking her beer from her and stealing a swig.

"Help yourself," came her sarcastic reply. "What do you care if they are staring?" One blond eyebrow shot way up and she continued before he could start his tirade. "I am going home with you. Unless you've changed your mind."

And she calms the savage beast. He grinned a predatory grin. "Not on your life, you are definitely coming home with me. Then you will just be coming." Still holding her beer in one of his hands he kissed her again, bending her backwards as the kiss deepened.

"There is a bed downstairs if you two need to use it," Terry's deep voice broke in.

Hot and bothered, they drew apart. With a wink Scott gave her back her beer and swaggered off, leaving her sagging against the rail of the ship. "Maybe later," he said as he headed over to where the men were still staring at her. "Y'all need to quit lookin' at my woman," Scott growled.

Chapter Thirteen

They spent the afternoon swimming, diving, and just having tons of all-around fun. Alexis was down in the main cabin attempting to fix the side tie of her bikini bottom. Dropping the skimpy sarong over the back of a chair, she froze as she heard the lock engage on the door. Turning around, she came face to face with one very handsome man named Scott. Her body prickled as his eyes moved over her nearly bare body.

"Took you long enough to come down here," he murmured as his large body flowed effortlessly towards hers.

"What are you doing in here?" Alexis asked, her gaze taking in his tanned muscular physique that was clothed solely in a pair of black swimming trunks.

"Waiting for you," he stated bluntly.

Her hands fell to the knot at the side of her bikini and she began to retie it as she spoke. "Why were you waiting for me?" *Who cares? He was waiting for you. YOU!*

Suddenly his hands were there brushing hers away. "I'll do it." He began to tie a knot for her. "I wanted to have you to myself for a while. I'm tired of sharing you."

Eyebrows raised, Alexis waited as he finished fixing her suit. "Well, here I am."

Hands settled around her ribcage, turning her body completely towards his. "Yes, here you are." He moved his gaze up and down her toasted skin. "This suit is killing me. I'm walking around up there with a hard-on because of this suit of yours." His lower body showed her he spoke the truth as he pressed it against her bare belly.

"Oh, so it's my fault?" Her eyes sparkled as her fingers danced across the skin on his arms.

"No one else on this boat can get this reaction from me." His hips bucked lightly against her.

"So, perhaps you were thinking of whoever can." Alexis' stone grew sharp while her fingers stilled.

Scott shook his head. "Don't overanalyze what I say, my sexy healer. You are the only woman I can't control myself around." His fingers brought her face around towards his from where she had been glancing across the room.

"Does that include Stacey?" Her eyes were direct as they stared into his.

He grinned. "Are you jealous of her?" His hands slid around the back of her neck, untying the knot that kept up the material that covered, however barely, her full breasts.

"Yes," she answered candidly.

The strings fell from her neck, exposing her naked torso to the blond man before her. "Don't be." His callused hands cupped her breasts, his thumbs moving over already tight nipples. "You are the woman I want." He lightly pinched her nipples. "The *only* woman I want."

Alexis's back arched, pressing her breasts further into his waiting hands, as a purr emerged from her mouth. "She's in love." Eyes darkened by desire met Scott's.

Without missing a beat he responded. "Too bad for her. I am too. My heart has already been claimed by another." His firm lips latched onto one taut nipple, drawing it into the heat of his mouth.

Knees trembled at the contact. Alexis bit back a moan as her hands pressed his head even tighter to her breast. "Does she know that?" She fought to stay focused on her questions.

His captivating mouth moved from one breast to the other with his tongue tracing the path between them. Dropping one hand, Scott cupped her ass as his fingers slipped beneath the skimpy material to caress her silken skin. "I don't know and I will tell her, but later. I have something else in mind right now." His words vibrated her whole nipple, sending wave after wave of electrical impulses through her body.

Alexis didn't care about anything else anymore. The man making love to her with his mouth could make her forget everything. And she did. Forgotten was the fact everyone knew where they were and what they were doing, the fact she was destroying the dream of a young woman. Everything except Scott and his magical touch on her licentious body.

※

A young woman wiped away tears from her dark face as she left her private room. By the time she reached the upstairs deck, there was no evidence that she'd just been devastated by the man she had always wanted to marry. That her lifelong fantasy had been shattered. Her smiles were forced as she rejoined her father's friends.

※

Scott laid them both down on the thick carpet, his mouth still drawing heavily on her breast. The hand that had been on her firm butt slid around to rest over the small, neatly trimmed patch of hair between her legs.

Alexis couldn't stay silent any longer and a seductive groan filled the room. Her body ached for him. "Please," she begged.

"What do you want, Lex?" His fingers parted the lips between her legs as his mouth moved up her body to nibble at the corner of hers. "Who does your body cry for?"

Lex. It makes me melt even more to hear him call me that. "I want you." She panted as her body rose, trying to encourage his fingers to penetrate. "I want to feel you inside me, Commander," she babbled, unable to think straight as his fingers moved over her mons with feather-like touches. "I want you. Please, Scott."

He drove two fingers home deep within her, capturing the scream of passion she released in his own mouth. "I want you too, Lex." Scott rose up so he was on his knees, bringing her with him. His thick fingers were still buried up to the knuckles within her.

The second she could, Alexis slid her hands into his pants, wrapping her fingers around his hard penis. Her action garnered a groan from Scott and his hips bucked, moving his erection through her tight grip.

Their lips met as they knelt on the floor of the yacht, the motion of the ocean adding its own push to their touches. Each rock of the boat caused them both to shudder from the position of the other's hand.

Alexis shifted her weight, causing them to fall backwards onto the floor. She was on top and she ground down hard on his fingers, enjoying the feel of him inside her to the fullest. Biting her lip, she rose off his chest and removed his fingers from her body. Her dark hair shook as she wordlessly told him no as he reached for her.

Grasping his shorts at the waist, Alexis slid off his body, bringing them with her. Her hand tossed them aside to land away from them. The hair on his legs brushed tantalizingly against her painfully tight nipples as she moved up his legs to place her mouth over his rampant erection.

Her tongue swirled over the swollen head, cleaning off the drops of moisture that were present before she drew the whole thing into her wet mouth. "Jesus, Lex!" he hissed to the room as his hips jumped up off the carpet, driving more of his substantial length into her waiting mouth.

Strong fingers circled around the base of his penis as her tongue coated his manhood with her saliva. As she stroked him, her mouth drew him into the warmth that sent him spiraling off towards an abyss. His hands clenched into fists as he tried to control the desire flowing freely in his blood.

Faster and harder she stroked, her mouth sucking unyieldingly on the stiff erection. Scott moaned aloud to the room, letting his hands sank into her thick hair, holding her in place as his hips began to buck harder. "Lex, stop," he begged.

Tiger eyes, heavy and sultry, drifted languidly up to meet his gaze. Her hand stopped moving as she waited for him to speak, running her tongue all over the head of his cock. Alexis shook her head slightly before sucking hard on the head without dropping his gaze. His lower body jerked while her mouth slid back down on his erection, taking more and more of it in.

Scott let go of her hair and sat up, looking down at the beautiful woman dressed only in Wedgewood-blue bikini bottoms who was giving him the blowjob of her life. His eyes kept fluttering closed as she alternated her strokes and sucks just enough to keep him on the edge of ejaculating but never allowing him to get there.

Without missing a beat, her free hand pushed on his chest, sending him back to the floor. That free hand found and flicked against one of his tight nipples, causing another tremor through his body.

Alexis kept him on the edge for a while longer. Scott seemed to have long since lost the ability to think straight or clearly. His eyes were squeezed closed as his hands had once again found their way into her hair, holding her where she was quite content to be.

"Please let me come, Lex," he groaned as she again drew him away from the edge of fulfillment.

So she did. Her hand around the shaft of his cock tightened and stroked him harder as her tongue teased the head. Finally, that hand fell away and Alexis slid her mouth and throat down over his entire erection and lightly ran her nails across his scrotum. Scott came with a fury and a shout.

Alexis moved back up his manhood and cleaned up any last remaining trace of his come with her tongue. Content with her job, she crawled up his body and settled herself over his still hard penis, slipping down until he was fully inside of her dripping wet body.

He rolled them over so she was on the bottom and he could pound her. Scott took in the woman beneath him. Her body was flushed, nipples hard pebbles, and sweat covered her body as she rose to meet each thrust he gave.

"Put your legs up," he ordered as his strokes continued. She immediately placed them over his shoulders, giving him better access to her depths. "Pinch your nipples for me." Alexis's eyes flew open at that but he just drilled into her harder. "Do it, Lex." When she did, the sight of her manicured fingers with their white tips holding her dusky hard nipples made him groan and pump his hips faster. "Don't let go until I tell you."

Lost in a haze of pleasure, Alexis didn't think about defying him. All she could feel was the pleasure that coursed through her body. He slowed down, his strokes almost stopping as he slid his length inside her only to pull it back until just the head remained. Her eyes narrowed at being denied her release.

"No, I didn't say to let go." His words penetrated her mind and she realized she'd been letting go of her nipples. As her fingers once again tightened around them, he rewarded her with a fast, hard, deep stroke.

Alexis hissed in pleasure—a hiss that turned into a groan as he slowed again. In and out he moved with deliberate, prolonged, and drawn-out motions. "Scott," she begged.

His eyes burned into her soul, unbeknownst to her, soldering them together even more. "What, my love?" His tongue trailed over her fingers and the nipples they held between them, sending another shudder through her.

"Love me," she cried as his hips seemed to go even slower.

"I do." Another pass of his tongue. "And I am." Again another pass, but this time his teeth grazed her nipple as he slammed into her. "Look at me," he commanded.

Somehow her eyes managed to open and focus on him. He kissed her lips before watching her as he moved within her. "You should see yourself, Lex," he murmured, his hips gaining some speed. "You are so beautiful lying there, pinching your own nipples, your legs over my shoulders."

All she could do was whimper. Her tongue darted out to lick her lips and Scott moved faster and harder. His fingers dug into the flesh of her hips and he held her still for his driving thrusts. "Let me hear your pleasure, Lex," he said, noticing her biting her lip to stay silent.

Her fingers tightened on their own, bringing herself even more pleasure as she dropped her head back and allowed her moans to escape. Alexis was barely able to maintain eye contact but she did, knowing he wanted her to.

The fire began to get even more intense inside her body as he drove deep into her. He dropped one hand from her hips and found her clit. Rolling it between his fingers he demanded, "Let go now." She released her nipples and was lost to a world of bright lights and stars as he slammed home one more time within her and coated her with his seed. His yell echoed hers.

Still buried inside her, Scott only just got her legs down before his body shuddered against hers and he lay over her. Hearts pounded out tattoos as the sweaty bodies remained on the carpeted floor.

Rolling to his back, Scott moved her to rest on his chest. The rocking of the yacht sent them both extra pleasure as they were still connected. His hands clasped behind her back and held her to him. Alexis had her ear pressed to his chest and she could hear the pounding of his heart. It matched hers. Her limbs felt boneless, she couldn't move. She didn't want to.

Five minutes passed before they both heard a knock at the door. "If y'all are done in there, we will be eating just as soon as the others get back from another dive." Terry's voice was easily recognizable.

Alexis's eyes flew open as her location just dawned on her. She scrambled off Scott and grabbed her bathing suit, heading for the private head in the room. Scott followed her and tied her bikini top on for her, pressing kisses all around her shoulders as he did so.

"What has you so worried, Lex?" he asked, meeting her gaze in the mirror.

"They all know what we have been doing. And for how long." A blush moved up her face.

"So? If I know Brian and Devón, they have found time to do the same thing with their women." He dropped her hair back down and smiled at her.

"They are married," she stated as if that should make it all clear.

He arched a brow. "Is that a proposal?"

YES! "Be serious. They are going to think I am such a slut."

His eyes hardened as his hands shook her gently but hard enough to get her attention. "No one is going to think that. Why are you feeling like this?"

To her horror, tears sprung in her eyes. "I just meet them and I am screwing you in a cabin on the boat that same day. They know how long we have known each other, for you told them."

"Alexis," Scott said calmly, wrapping his hands around her waist. "I told them I met you in Norfolk. For them that makes it two years ago. They all like you. Hell, I think the single guys are half in love with you themselves" He grumbled that last bit. "It's not like they would blame me for wanting to bring you down here to…" he paused, capturing and holding her gaze, "make love to you. Even Brian and Devón would understand."

"That doesn't matter, they are married. They can do this sort of thing." She moaned and dropped her gaze.

His fingers brought her chin up so she was meeting his eyes once again. His were clear and direct when he said, "So marry me."

Chapter Fourteen

Alexis carefully kept her expression neutral, though he saw her eyelashes flutter. "That's not funny, Commander," she said, leaving the bathroom, walking through the room and barely slowing to grab her sarong before unlocking the door and moving up the stairwell.

Scott was on her ass like green stuck to grass. Those gorgeous eyes of his had narrowed and his large body prevented her from proceeding. "I wasn't being funny, Alexis." He let loose a low growl. "And *stop* calling me Commander."

"I'm not marrying you. I can't marry you," she said in a controlled voice.

Now he knew what real pain felt like. *I'm not giving up that easily, Lex; you are going to have to do a hell of a lot better than that.* Scott opened his mouth to respond when a shout from the deck grabbed their attention.

"Stacey! Get out of there. Sharks are inbound!" Terry's voice was full of dread.

The conversation between them halted as they ran up the few stairs and to the side where Stacey was floundering in the water. Scott didn't even slow, his muscular body sailing over the edge and executing a perfect dive into the ocean. He resurfaced a short way away and began to knife effortlessly through the water towards the petrified girl.

As he reached her side, he could tell she'd truly begun to panic. "Calm down, Stacey."

Her dark eyes were wild with fear. "Sharks," she gurgled as she sank below the surface.

Scott was well aware of the increasing number of fins circling their location. Pulling her head back above water he said, "Hold still,

Stacey, thrashing is only going to excite them." Her flailing body only intensified its force. "Forgive me, Stacey." With one fast movement, he knocked her unconscious, and then he quickly maneuvered her body so it wouldn't sink beneath the surface as he towed her to the yacht.

"Harrier, two more coming at your three o'clock!" Terry yelled as the others fired shots into the water, trying to give Scott a clear path to the yacht.

Scott felt the bump as one shark "tested" him. "Get ready to pull her out!" he shouted, moving closer as another shark hit him.

Terry and Brian were ready to pull while the others had bang sticks and guns. The sharks were getting more aggressive with each stroke Scott took. Looking forward, Scott's concentrated gaze landed on Alexis who stood at the edge in her bikini holding an M-16 in her hands. *I love her.* Those words rang through his soul as he swam towards her.

"Two more coming up from back aft!" Tag shouted from where he stood watching the fish finder, waiting until Scott and Stacey were on safely back on board to drive the boat away. The anchor had already been weighed.

"Ready, guys?" Scott asked the two hanging over the side.

"Ready!" Terry said as Alexis released a burst of gunfire into the water nearby. The men jerked the still-unconscious girl into the boat. As soon as she was clear, Devón, Antwon, and Mario heaved Scott's larger, heavier body into the yacht.

Following right on his heels was the open jaw of a large shark. Seconds after its head was exposed, Alexis turned and emptied round after round into it until the lifeless body fell back into the water to be torn apart by the other sharks.

Dropping the gun, Alexis shifted into her doctor mode. Stacey would be fine. After the initial diagnosis, the men carried her carefully to the bed in her room and laid her upon it. Back up on deck, Alexis turned her attention to Scott who had a first aid kit open beside him.

"Are you okay?" she asked, taking the antiseptic wipe from him and tenderly cleaning his wounds.

"It's only a few abrasions," Scott said while her hand administered gently to him. "How's Stacey?"

She paused. "She will be fine. I think her worst injury will be to her pride. She is in her bed. Jakobie and Randi are with her if you want to sit with her."

Alexis kept her eyes on the raw abrasions he had gotten, and he thought that wouldn't do at all. "Look at me, Lex, my love." He tipped her face towards his with one finger.

"I have to go check on Stacey again. You'll be fine." She backed away and disappeared in a flash of beautiful ebony skin.

Terry sat beside Scott as the rest of the men gathered around as well. "Thank you so much, Harrier. I don't know what I would do if I lost my little girl. Are you sure you're all right?"

"I'm fine, Terry. Fine," Scott assured his friend.

"I don't know what in the hell made her do something this stupid. She was raised on the water; she knows what the dangers are."

"It's over, man," Scott said.

"No, she could have been killed. You could have been killed. This was some sort of stunt that went horribly wrong."

"She's in love with Scott," Alexis's voice cut in. All the men looked at her and the two women behind her. "She's awake." Terry stood but sat back down when she added, "Stacey wants to see Harrier."

Immediately, Scott stood and headed for the stairs, stopping briefly before Alexis who'd just stepped back and let him pass. As he walked down the steps he heard Alexis say, "Well, I could use a drink. And I believe someone said something about dinner. I'm hungry."

Tag's teasing voice followed him down the stairs. "I bet. After being downstairs with Harrier, I know y'all worked up an appetite!"

Scott kept going although he wanted nothing more than to go back and give Tag a piece of his mind. Knocking on the door, Scott went in at the subdued "Enter" that filtered through the wood. Inside the room he saw Stacey lying in her bed under the covers. She still looked pale and shaken up.

"Hey, Sport," Scott said, sitting on the edge of her bed. "How are you doing?"

"Okay, I guess. Embarrassed, ashamed, and exhausted." Her eyes were still wide as they watched him.

"What were you doing, Stacey? You almost gave me a heart attack."

"You do care about me," she gushed, readjusting herself on the bed so her head was on one of his granite thighs.

"Of course I do." *Why did Alexis move away from me before I came down here?* His mind was focused on the woman up on deck as opposed to the young one beside him.

"I saw you didn't even hesitate when you jumped in to save me. You love me, don't you." It was a statement not a question.

Scott heard all of Alexis's words about Stacey having feelings for him and realized she was right. He'd just thought she was jealous of Stacey. "Is that why you jumped overboard?"

"I knew you were lying to *that woman* you were with in Daddy's room. You want me instead of her." Stacey cuddled closer and tried to slip her arms around him.

He froze for a second, stunned beyond belief that she would actually believe that. Scott got off the bed and sat on a chair facing her. "Stacey, listen to me and listen well." He waited for her eyes to meet his. "You are very special to me. And you always will be, but I love you like you were one of my own. I have known you since you were two and a half."

"To me, you and your father are family. But I have no romantic feelings for you at all. None. I wasn't lying to Alexis, she holds the key, *the only key*, to my heart. I am in love with her." Scott watched as his words sank in.

"You don't even know her!" Stacey cried.

"I've known her for two years. I can't ignore what my heart is telling me," he said gently.

She pouted. "What about my heart?"

"I think your heart is holding onto a childhood crush. Nothing more. Are you telling me there is no one who has caught your eye at school?" he asked, arching a brow.

"They are all boys. I want a man," she revealed. "I want you, Harrier. I've been in love with you for as long as I can remember. You are the one that I compare all other men to. I know you would feel the same if you would just give it a chance," the young woman pled.

"I will always be there for you, Stacey, and love you, but there will never be an 'us'."

"I hate her!" Stacey spat.

Scott might not be the wisest man when it came to matters dealing with the "fairer" sex, but he sure knew who Stacey meant. "Don't say that," he ordered in a hard voice.

"But you were supposed to marry me!" Stacey whined, pounding her fists on the mattress.

"I'm sorry, Stacey, that you somehow got that impression. You will find the right man one day." Scott retook a seat on the bed, this time sitting beside her, slipping one strong arm around her shoulders.

"I wanted you to be that man." Her suddenly solemn voice was barely over a whisper.

A gentle smile crossed his face. "Darlin', you don't want me. I am fifteen years older than you. You want a man who shares your interests, your desires. And I will be right there with your father, scaring the crap out of him when that day comes."

"I am so sorry for my actions today." Stacey laid her head on his shoulder. "I just wanted you to see me in trouble, to rescue me, and realize how much you loved me."

"Oh, Stacey. Promise me you won't do anything like this again. And when we get upstairs, make sure you apologize to your father."

"Do you hate me?" she asked quietly.

"No. I could never hate you." He brushed a kiss over her forehead. "I will *always* love you."

"I will always love you, too, Harrier."

Neither of them witnessed the woman walk silently back up the steps, her own feelings conflicted at the emotional words she'd heard between the two people in the small cabin room.

※

By the time Scott and Stacey made it up to the outside deck, the party was back into full swing. Music poured out of the speakers and folks munched through the large spread of food and drink. Alexis and Tag were dancing together in the sunset.

Stacey apologized to everyone individually after speaking to her father and soon the incident was behind them as people began to eat and drink more. Scott walked over towards the dancing couple, trying hard not to be jealous. "Mind if I steal her for a bit, Tag?"

"Of course I mind, but since I don't want you to kick my ass, I will back off. Another dance later, my dear?" he asked as he kissed the back of Alexis's hand.

"Definitely, Tag," her velvet voice responded as she smiled at him. "What?" Alexis asked after Scott directed her to a spot that was a bit more secluded.

"Thanks for everything you did today, for Stacey especially." Scott stood there looking down at the woman whose features where highlighted by the soft light of the setting sun. Her eyes were expressionless and it scared him.

"You're welcome. Is that it?"

"What the hell has happened since we made love in the cabin to change your attitude so much?" he snapped.

She shrugged, not meeting his eyes. "Nothing. I just want to put on my shirt and pants."

"Let's go then." He gestured for her to lead the way.

Wordlessly, she walked into the room and went straight to her clothes, slipping them on over her now-dry bikini, covering up her amazing body even more. "Excuse me," she said, stopping in front of him since he was blocking the door.

"Lex, talk to me. Baby," he coaxed. "What's wrong?" One hand reached for her face, but his heart still shattered as her soft smile didn't reach up to her exotic eyes.

"Nothing," she insisted even though she knew they both knew that was a lie. "I want to enjoy time on deck with our friends. And watch the evening arrive."

Scott did know she loved watching sunsets so he moved aside. Alexis slipped past him and was back at the party before he could decide on his next thought.

As the yacht pulled into its designated slip, everyone was tired. It had been a full day. Alexis had been flirtatious and fun with all the guests and only Scott knew something was missing from her seemingly joyous attitude.

Walking off the boat with Terry and Tag, Alexis had a grin on her face. "Thank you so much for letting me be a part of the group."

"Sweetheart, anytime you want, you are welcome on board," Terry said.

"Well, as tempting as the offer is, I'm stationed on the other coast. But if I'm ever back this way...I'll take you up on it," Alexis said as she kissed his dark cheek.

"What about me?" Tag jokingly asked.

With a wink to Terry she said, "Well, okay, I'll move so you can kiss him too!"

The trio burst out laughing as Tag slid his arm around her shoulders. "Not what I meant."

"I sure figured on you being out on this coast," Terry said as they walked up the pier.

"Why?" she questioned, looking between both men.

"Harrier," they answered simultaneously.

Brows furrowed as she fought the urge to look over her shoulder at that very man. "Explain please." Her voice somehow managed to stay modulated.

Terry spoke first. "He has never brought a woman here on the boat with us. When he would date someone, he always told them it was 'guys only'. Then Devón brought Jakobie, eventually they were married, and then the same with Brian and Randi. So you must be something special to him. I almost fell over when he said he was bringing a date."

Tag took over. "We meet a few times a year, and for a long time it was only Stacey, Jakobie, and Randi as the women on the boat. Have you met his Team yet?"

"A few times on the carrier. After a mission," she said.

"Let me guess," Tag conjectured. "He waits for you to check him over."

Maybe. "It just happened that way," Alexis protested. Both men laughed, looked back at Harrier, and laughed again. "Guys, come on," she begged.

"He has got it bad. Not that I blame him." Tag hugged her with the arm around her shoulders. "Welcome to the family, hon. Welcome to our family."

"You have it all wrong," she tried again.

"Nope," they both stated immediately. "He has a radar lock on you, girl," Terry added, sounding positively gleeful.

Alexis kept her mouth shut since Scott had walked up to them, dislodging Tag's arm and putting his own there. "I'll thank y'all not to fill my lovely little healer's head with stories."

"So I shouldn't believe what they were telling me?" Alexis wondered as she instinctively leaned into him.

"Depends," he purred, sending pulse after pulse of desire through her. "Only believe what makes me more impressive to you."

"Well, then, I can't believe anything they said," she teased as her hand found its way into the pocket of his jeans.

Halting at the end of the pier, the group said farewells. As Tag hugged her he murmured in a stage whisper, "Whenever you want a *real* man, let me know."

"Tag!" the barely-contained roar came. "Get the hell away from my woman!"

His woman. She was so conflicted about the feelings he stirred inside her. With a quick hug, Alexis stepped back from Tag and immediately found herself hauled up against the hard physique of the one Navy SEAL who had captured her heart.

"Goodnight all. I am going to take her home before one more man presses his lips to her. Y'all have no sense of boundaries," Scott grumbled playfully—sort of.

"Until we meet again, Dr. Lex," Terry said with a wink as she waved a farewell and was led back to the Corvette that sat under a lamppost by the man who was madly in love with her.

Chapter Fifteen

Scott opened the door for the woman tucked into the side of his body. "You know you are eventually gonna have to tell me what's wrong," he said in his resonating timbre as he helped Alexis into the car.

"Nothing's wrong," Alexis insisted.

"You shouldn't lie to your future husband," he growled in her ear, making sure her door was securely shut.

"I'll keep that in mind for when I meet him," she retorted, watching him out of the corner of her eye.

His body rippled as he flexed his muscles and tried to remain in control of his emotions. *You have met him, and I'll be damned if I let some other man touch any part of your delicious body.* "Your firm ass is sitting in his car right now," Scott grumbled. He vaulted over the driver-side door, landing gracefully in the seat.

Her tiger eyes widened at his effortless movement. "Perhaps you aren't as well as I first thought. Maybe you shouldn't drive."

"Oh, I'm fine." His intense gaze swung over to meet her half-skeptical, half-amused one. "And I wasn't joking." Scott started the Corvette and drove off into the night.

Biting her lower lip, Alexis watched him, but he stayed focused on the road. "Weren't joking about what?" she asked, playing dumb.

Scott knew it. With a mild curse, he jerked the car off the road and killed the engine. Before Alexis could say a word she was straddling his lap, her butt resting on the steering wheel. "About us," he snarled before his mouth claimed hers in a dominating kiss.

His tongue demanded entrance and turned her body into a quivering mass of hormones. Scott's large hands grabbed her ass and squeezed as he continued to preside over the kiss. Small whimpers moved up her throat and she pressed herself down over his rapidly hardening erection. Her pelvis rocked back and forth, driving them both closer to the edge.

Leaving her ass, his hands grabbed her hair and pulled her head back, separating their mouths. The moon offered the only light as they sat on that deserted stretch of road. "Do you know how much it hurts to have you doubt my feelings?" he ground out.

"Do you have any idea how it feels to me to hear you tell another woman you will always love her?" came her own hissed response.

Well, now I know what made her attitude change. She overheard me talking to Stacey. "I don't want Stacey." *I know you love me, Alexis, you have to.* "Oh, God, Lex, I'd marry you right now if you'd let me. I want a family, I want a family with you." His lips pressed against hers as he spoke. "I want to know that you are mine to love, mine to hold, and just, well, just mine." Scott didn't even bother to hide the anguish in his voice.

She sighed and held him tighter. "Take me home and make love to me," she muttered against his mouth.

With one last, long, soul-drugging kiss, Scott lifted her back over to her side of the car. In moments, they were driving back towards his cabin, hands still touching as if breaking contact would somehow shatter the spell they were under.

Whipping into the yard, Scott had bounded from the car before the engine had totally died and was around to her side of the car, lifting her bodily out and carrying her to the door. He held her as she unlocked the door to the cabin.

Alexis slammed the door shut behind them as Scott pressed his lips back to hers. He maneuvered through the dark house toward his bedroom, where he longed to lay his woman down and love her like she deserved. Her arms wound trustingly around his neck as he took the stairs without hesitation.

It was with the utmost care that Scott laid Alexis upon the bed. He removed her clothes and then his. Her skin, which had been momentarily chilled from the ocean breeze, was warmed once again as the raw power of Harrington Prescott Broderick Leighton III settled over her, pressing her into the mattress.

Only the moonlight filtering through the curtains was allowed witness to the expressions of love that they shared throughout the rest of the night.

※

Damn. Damn. Damn. Damn! Alexis swore to herself as she watched the cabbie placed her last suitcase in the trunk of the taxi.

"Ready when you are, ma'am," the driver said as he climbed back behind the wheel.

"Right." With one last longing glance at the house and then down to the beach, Alexis gripped the handle of the door. There was still no sign of the man she was hoping to see.

Opening the door, she was just about to slide across the seat when she heard a man yelling, "Wait! Lex, what the hell is going on here? Where are you going?" Scott was running up the path, sweaty from his jog.

"Just give me a minute," she said to the driver before turning to meet the handsome SEAL partway.

"What is going on?" Scott was furious and panicked.

"I waited as long as I could—" Alexis began.

"You have only been here for three days. Don't run away from what we have, Lex. Stay. Stay here with me." His eyes searched hers.

"I left a note for you inside on the breakfast bar." Twice she reached for him only to pull back and ball her hand up into a fist.

"A note. You left me a note. I leave you sleeping in bed and you were going to leave me a note?" He was incredulous.

Her eyes met his without flinching. "I was recalled. I have to go."

She heard him curse under his breath. "Do you want to?" Those four words were asked in a quiet voice as he twirled a loose tendril of her hair around two fingers.

"No." *I don't ever want to leave you.* Heedless of the sweat covering his body, she reached around his neck and hugged him tight. "Thank you for the best vacation I ever had, Harrington Prescott Broderick Leighton the Third, even if it was cut short." Her words were whispered into his ear.

Arms of steel encircled her curvaceous body as his lips teased the skin behind her ear. "Thank you." Pulling back so he could see her face, he sent her a smile that turned her bones to mush. With a kiss that embraced both of their souls, he said his farewell.

"Goodbye, Commander," Alexis said as she stepped back from his touch.

Scott walked with her to the cab and held the door as she began to climb in. When her golden eyes looked up at him from where she sat; he knelt down so they were at eyelevel. Oblivious to the voyeuristic gaze of the driver, he captured her face within both his hands.

His thumbs skimmed lightly over the lips he had just kissed and his fingers played in the silkiness of her hair. Scott kissed her one last lingering time, draining her body of support. Moving slightly back until he could look into her eyes, he held her gaze and spoke. "I love you, Alexis Milele Rogets. I will always love you." Another kiss and he was gone and she was being driven out of his life.

Chapter Sixteen

"General quarters! General quarters!" The horn blared along with that damn grating voice. "Damn it all to hell!" Alexis swore as she scrambled out of her rack and away from the best sex she'd had since her vacation three months ago. Of course, she'd expect it to be great, for even in her dreams it was still Commander Leighton who piloted her to the stars and beyond.

Two hours later, she'd been granted permission to disembark the ship at the port where they were docked. Walking with another woman from the *Everett*, she strolled along the streets of Hong Kong and enjoyed browsing through the items for sale in the numerous stands.

"I will be so glad when we are back home," Katie, who was also a chief, said.

"Me too. I want the rest of my vacation," Alexis complained. *Take me away from the best sex I had in my life. Damn it all!*

Katie chuckled. "I would, too, if I was with a hot man." She winked. "Who was this mysterious man who rocked your world?"

"I never should have told you about that. And we both know that you have hot men all the time." And it was true; Katie was a beautiful, voluptuous golden-skinned woman of Spanish descent and had that dark coloring that could drive men wild...and did.

"Honey, you could have just as many if you wanted. In fact, you do have as many; you could have more if you would just flirt."

I had the best man there ever will be. "My life is full enough with Jay and this gig. I sure don't need no man trying to control me."

Sliding her arm through Alexis's, Katie stated, "No, what you need is a man's man to spirit you away, tie you up, and do horribly wicked and wonderful things to you with chocolate sauce and edible oils."

Alexis remembered Scott and whipped cream. With a shuddering breath she teased, "That sounds like your kind of man, Katie." *Remember what it was like to lick whipped cream off his...?*

"Oh, Lex, don't be a prude!"

More and more images of making love with Scott in the cabin on the yacht flooded her memory. *I don't think I am a prude!* "I will always be a prude compared to you. Now, let's go eat. I'm hungry for some good food."

Laughing, the two friends went and ate at a sidewalk café. Lex and Katie were hopelessly unaware of the hazel eyes watching them before their owner flipped open a phone and made a call.

By the time the meal was over, Alexis was stuffed. "Now I remember why everyone always takes a siesta after lunch," she groaned, clasping her hands over her belly.

"Please," her friend scoffed. "You need to eat more. You are getting too skinny."

Alexis just rolled her eyes. "I am the same size as you." She arched a brow. "My clothes are just a bit bigger.

"I know, I wear them," Katie admitted, which just got a look that said "duh" from Alexis.

The women walked on, joining more people from their ship as well as the carrier *Endeavor*. The large group entered a dance club and grabbed a table and drinks.

"God, I've missed this," Alexis said over the loud music.

"Come on, let's dance!" Katie grabbed her arm and led them out on the floor. Alexis was totally enjoying herself when she felt a tingle down her spine. It was almost as if someone were watching her. She shook her head, however, telling herself she was imagining things and let herself have a good time.

Four hours later, Alexis was done. She wanted to catch some rack time. Waving to Katie and the rest of the group, she turned her exhausted body towards the door and slipped out, unaware three figures followed her down the street.

Before Alexis turned the corner a male voice yelled, "Lex!" The men following her swiftly ducked into the shadows and watched.

Turning quickly, Lex honed in on the person who had bellowed for her. A brilliant smile crossed her face as she ran towards the man. "Piers!" she screeched, launching herself into his embrace and placing a kiss on his lips.

The man was tall, dark-skinned, and very muscular. He hugged her tightly. "Why didn't you tell me you were here?" he demanded, setting her on her feet only to place a thick arm around her shoulders.

"We just got in today. What about you?" she asked in a delighted tone.

"Come back with me to my hotel room and we will catch up."

"Works for me, I was just on my way back to my rack. So a real bed sounds great." Her arm slid around his trim waist with a comfortable and familiar action.

A body rigid with anger watched as the couple walked off arm in arm.

※

Two nights later...

"Wow, Lex, you look great!" The man waiting for her at the hotel lobby said with a long whistle.

Alexis wore a dark indigo formal dress that fit her curvaceous form tightly all the way down. A long slit went up the left side, exposing flashes of one very smooth, sepia leg. Her three-inch heels put her closer to the height of the man escorting her.

"Thanks, Piers. I wasn't sure I was going to find something. This isn't exactly what's normally in my sea bag." They walked from the hotel to the waiting limo and climbed in.

He chuckled. "Well, you look amazing."

"You don't look so bad yourself there." Piers wore a tux that was handmade to drape perfectly over his muscular frame.

The ride to their destination was of companionable silence as Alexis looked out the window at their surroundings.

"Wow," she breathed. "This is amazing." The limo pulled up in front of an enormous and spectacular pagoda-style mansion.

With a smile, Piers led them into the grand ballroom where there were formally dressed people everywhere. "Ready to schmooze?" he teased.

Alexis laughed. "Oh, no. You are the schmoozer. I'm just the schmoozer's date." Her eyes took in military uniforms, both foreign and domestic, tuxedos, and very expensive dresses. She smiled her thanks at the waiter who gave her a flute of champagne and began to mingle with her date.

Two hours later, Alexis stood on a stone balcony off the second floor overlooking the twinkling lights of the portside city. "This view is unbelievable. I love it," she murmured, running a finger over the smooth alabaster marble.

"I agree; this balcony offers a perfect view." A velvet whisper broke through her peace.

Alexis just about fainted, not from fright, but from the raw emotions that poured into her body. Scott. Commander Leighton. Turning, she laid her eyes on the real version of her fantasies…which, consequently, only increased after their time together. She couldn't say a word.

"Hello, Lex," he purred in his deep, seductive timbre.

She couldn't believe how much she wanted to run into his arms, to feel his lips upon her body. Before her bedazzled brain could form a coherent thought, Piers called to her from inside and with a single longing look, she just slipped away.

※

Scott swore a round of curses that would shock his SEAL team. From the second he'd gotten Tyson's call, he had been on her six, shadowing her, wanting to ignore the fact he was a superior officer and kiss her senseless like she was his whole world. And she was.

The Megalodon Team was in Hong Kong to keep an eye on the proceedings going on at one of the wealthy homes. However, Scott was spending all of his free time following his sexy little healer as she moved around town.

He'd seen her first at the club, and after three months, she'd still been a sight for sore eyes. She had been out on the floor dancing, her full hips swaying before his eyes like she were a snake charmer and he were the cobra in a basket. As he'd watched from the sidelines unseen, she'd danced freely and expressively with different partners, always, however, keeping within sight of shipmates.

The moment she'd walked out into the night, he'd planned on approaching her. With him in civilian clothes, no one would have recognized him in the dark and it wouldn't have mattered they were of different ranks.

That plan had gone to shit the second she'd had her attention grabbed by the handsome black man she'd called Piers. It had killed him to watch *his woman* run so easily into another man's arms. Two of his teammates had had to hold him from running out there when the man had suggested going back to his hotel and she'd accepted.

The next day he couldn't leave his post to follow her and find out who that man was. Scott had called the *Everett* to find out how long they were in port and had finagled a trip home with them instead of staying on the *Endeavor*.

Then this morning, Scott had found Alexis once she'd left the ship only to meet that Piers man and go off with him. Scott had followed their steps but didn't understand what was said, for they'd been speaking Spanish fluently.

Unfortunately, Scott had to abandon his scouting to go to his hotel and get ready for this evening. Part of him, the primitive part, had wanted to dig and find out about the unknown man, but he hadn't. Scott was determined to talk to her first and give her a chance to explain.

He'd arrived to the gala before Alexis, but when he'd finally seen her, Scott had been blown away. Her entire body was dressed in a sinful wrapping, and for the first time in his life, Scott had run away. He'd gotten almost used to the feelings she evoked in him: frustration, lust, anger, desire, joy. Even the fantasies, daydreams, and heart-racing moments had become old hat to him. The jealousy he could deal with, to a certain extent. But the force of love that had hit him tonight scared him.

He'd known for a long time now how he felt, but Scott had not been prepared for the intensity of those feelings. When he'd seen her before in Hong Kong, part of him had always been focused on the man at her side and trying to control his temper, but tonight...tonight he couldn't see anything beyond the indigo dress that caressed Alexis's body so perfectly. Yet when he'd approached her during a moment when she'd finally been alone, she'd fled, firming his resolve to talk to her.

"I don't think so, my Nubian healer. I'm not about to let you get away that easily." Scott drained the rest of his drink in one gulp and straightened his perfectly-creased uniform before walking back into the building.

Walking down the stairs, Scott's sharp gaze picked out the object of his desire. Currently she stood with a few other officers, some he knew and some he didn't. It didn't matter, though, for they were all looking at her too lecherously.

One of the men flagged him down as he approached. "Commander, you must come meet this woman."

Bold blue eyes swept over her body as he walked up to the group. "Gentleman," Scott said smiling at them all. "Ma'am."

"Alexis, this is Commander Leighton. Commander, this is—"

Reaching for her hand, he shook it as he interrupted, "Chief Rogets. We've met. A pleasure to see you again." His index finger trailed along the inside of her wrist as he allowed her to take back possession of her hand.

"Commander," she said in her husky voice, nodding slightly. "Good to see you again as well." The tip of her tongue slipped out to moisten her full lips, drawing his eyes to them. "Good to see you gentlemen, also, but I think I need to go find my date. Excuse me." Just as earlier, she melted away, leaving Scott frustrated and horny.

Hell, no! "Excuse me as well, gentlemen, there is a matter that I must discuss with Chief Rogets." He was gone before they could say anything one way or the other.

"Chief Rogets, may I have a word?" Scott's deep voice broke into her conversation with another man she was talking to.

"Of course, Commander. Excuse me, Señor Padilla," Alexis said politely.

"Not a problem, we will talk again later, no?" He kissed the back of her hand and walked away.

She turned those expressive eyes onto Scott asking, "What can I do for you, Commander?"

"I think this is best done in private." He gestured towards the door and the labyrinth.

With all the bearing of royalty, she turned and walked ahead of him. She waited in silence until he stopped her with a touch and crowded her towards the corner where they were completely obstructed from view. For all intents and purposes they were alone; they would hear anyone coming before they got there.

"What is it, Commander?" Alexis asked again, looking at him politely.

"This." She was in his arms in a second, her mouth devoured by a starving man. His tongue swept deep into her mouth, experiencing again what he had already come to know and love.

Alexis purred contentedly as she arched into him. Her arms slid up his hard chest until her right hand touched his medals. She tensed immediately and drew away.

"Don't do that again," she hissed at him.

"Didn't you miss me, my love?" he asked, ignoring her statement and pulling her in closer until he was content with the miniscule distance separating them.

"This isn't your cabin; we can't do this," she protested, not giving him the answer he wanted to hear.

"We aren't even in the States, my seductive little healer. Or on a military installation." His thumbs moved tenderly over her bottom lip.

"The rules don't change just because we aren't in the country."

"No more talking." He captured her mouth with a gentle kiss, exploring her mouth like it was new and uncharted territory, his tongue dancing a slow seductive tango with hers.

Their tastes became blended. No more individual flavor, they were one. Two halves of the same whole.

Unable to resist, Alexis gave into his long, drugging kiss. Scott hoped she'd dreamed about his touch since she had climbed in the taxi and left him in front of his cabin the same way he'd dreamed of hers. Needing her closer, Scott slid his arms around her waist and picked her up off the ground.

"Stop, Commander!" she begged.

With a heavy sigh, he set her back on the ground, refrained from kissing her, but refused to stop touching her body. "I've missed you," he blurted out as two fingers ran down a corkscrew curl that framed her face.

"I've missed you too," she admitted as one of her fingers ran over the large swathe of decorations on his chest.

Those words lifted a huge weight off of his shoulders. "You still owe me four days."

She trembled at what that could entail. "I can't take any more time. We are leaving soon and this is a special chit request to come here with Piers."

Piers. Blue eyes narrowed before a very controlled question came. "Is he important to you?"

"Of course he is." Alexis cocked her head to the side. "Why wouldn't he be?"

"And you make it a habit to go to the hotel rooms of men in ports you visit?" His question was harsh and totally lacking in the care that had been there before.

"No, of course not," she exclaimed stunned. Her eyes narrowed in the moonlight. "How did you know I went to his…?" Alexis trailed off before her voice grew sharp and accusatory. "You bastard! What are you doing, following me? And you think I am like that?"

"I saw you around a few times," he tried, realizing that he had grieved egregiously.

"Around a few times, huh?" Her body was rigid as she stepped away fro him. "But you were close enough to me to hear my conversation with Piers?"

Shit, I stepped in it this time. "I was on my way—"

"Forget it, Commander," she snapped, slashing her hand through the air. "I don't owe you any explanations. Leave me alone!"

He reached for her but she eluded his grasp and moved away from him, keeping a particular distance between them as they left the labyrinth. Before she moved onto the lighted path, she stopped and glared at him so harshly he could feel the daggers. "Not that it is any of your concern, but Piers is my second-oldest brother." Spinning around in righteous anger, she stomped up the path and walked out of his life again.

Her brother? "When will I learn to keep my fucking mouth shut?" he swore as he allowed her to escape, for he wasn't about to do anything to embarrass her at this gathering.

For the rest of the night Lieutenant Commander Leighton mingled with the dignitaries and did his job. But always in his sights moved a beautiful dark-skinned doctor dressed, in his mind, mouthwateringly in an indigo dress. She managed to avoid him for the rest of the night without appearing to do so.

Chapter Seventeen

Sitting at the table, Alexis just pushed her food around on her plate. She hadn't had much of an appetite since she saw Commander Leighton at the pagoda in Hong Kong. Her feelings for him were still just as strong as they had always been. To be fair to him, it was possible that he didn't know the names of all her siblings; she didn't know all of his.

"Lex," the voice intruded. She looked up to see Katie waving her hand at her. "You okay, girl?"

Alexis smiled. "Fine, just not really hungry. I'm gonna go catch up on some reading." She stood and carried her tray to the conveyor belt leading to the kitchens. Waving over her shoulder, Alexis left the mess, and walked to her small area that held her meager possessions on the ship. Just as she lay down on her rack with a book, it happened.

"Chief Rogets report to medical! Chief Rogets report to medical!" The order came blaring over the loudspeaker.

Without hesitation, she rolled out of her small bed and swiftly navigated the narrow passageways to sick bay where she saw two men on examination tables. "What is going on here?" she demanded as she closed the door behind her.

"They fell down the ladders," the corpsman said with a shake of his head.

She attended the two men with lightheartedness and good humor. Finally she was done and decided once she returned to her quarters she'd sleep; it was too late for reading. Alexis was slipping back through the halls when she saw the captain and some others walking in her direction. Pressing herself against the wall to give them the right of way, she immediately recognized the scent of the man who brushed up against her.

"Sorry," that deep voice crooned as a hand reached out to touch her arm in apology.

"No problem, Commander," she said, refusing to look him in the eyes. His fingers stayed almost too long on her arm, but he dropped them before anyone could become suspicious. "Sirs," Alexis acknowledged before slipping off down the passageway, willing the beating of her heart not to give her away.

It wasn't a fulfilling sleep that claimed Alexis. Her dreams were nothing but Scott accusing her of being a whore. She awoke with a start to see Katie standing over her. "Lex," she said, extremely concerned. "Are you okay?"

Climbing carefully out of her rack, Alexis nodded. "Just a nightmare." she tried for a grin. "Thanks for waking me."

"Girl, you had me worried." Her dark expressive eyes moved over the unusually pale and drawn face of her good friend. "Oh, by the way, Touchette sent me to get you. He asked where you were and I said in your rack sleeping. He said that once you were awake to go to the officers' mess."

Squinting at the onset of a headache, Alexis nodded again. "When was that? How long ago?"

"About an hour or so. He said he knew you had just been on for twelve so if he wasn't in the mess, he would be in his room," Katie said, handing over a bottled water.

All Alexis could think about was Scott being on board the *Everett*. *Why wouldn't he be on the Endeavor? Because he wants to see you, Lex, ol' girl!* Taking a healthy gulp of water, she sighed. "Well, since I'm up I guess I should go." Alexis quickly braided her hair into a French braid and put her cap on.

With one quick look to make sure her uniform was acceptable, she sat down, tied on her boots, and looked up at Katie, who was waiting for her with a bemused expression on her face. "What?" she asked in Spanish as her eyes moved up to meet her friend's.

"Just thinking about those handsome SEALs we took onboard. It should be a *very* nice trip back with them around," Katie answered, also speaking Spanish.

A nice trip to hell! "They're just men, Katie. Wipe your mouth; you are drooling all over the floor," Alexis said semi-playfully, pleased that her voice was as it usually would be.

With one last sigh, Alexis rose and the women walked together, conversing in Spanish as they navigated the passageways. She knew they passed Scott because she felt that funny tremble inside her belly that he never failed to cause. Refusing to meet his gaze, she continued straight to find the captain who was waiting for her.

※

It had been five days since he and his Team had boarded the *Everett*, and Scott couldn't believe how well Alexis was managing to avoid him. On a carrier, her evasive maneuvers would be one thing, but this ship was much smaller than that. With a last look around, he swore as he left the flight deck and headed towards the officers' mess to fill his belly.

Walking behind two seamen, he overheard them talking about how nice HMC Rogets was. The deep, yearning urge to see her almost buckled his knees. It was time to go get some medical attention.

Ignoring the rumbling in his stomach, Scott turned and made his way to the private office for the doctor on duty. He knocked on the door, not exactly sure what to say. Scott didn't even know if she was on right now or not.

Knock. Knock. Knock.

"Come on in," Alexis called loudly through the door. Scott entered to see her back toward him, working on the computer. At the sound of the door closing, she still hadn't turned. "Just a moment and I'll be right with you. Have a seat."

He followed her directive, his blue eyes never leaving her form. He watched as Alexis logged off and spun around to talk to whomever needed her attention with a smile on her face. "What can I do for—" She faltered when she finally laid eyes on him.

"Chief," came the respectful tone even though his eyes removed every stitch of clothing he could see on her. *I can't lose you, Lex. I won't lose you!*

"Commander." She straightened her shoulders. "What can I do for you?"

"I need some medical advice," he said, leaning back in the chair and touching his fingertips together as his gaze held hers.

Her eyes grew to a rich honeyed color, but then she cleared her throat and blinked a few times. "Okay. What's the problem?"

The problem is we aren't married. "Well, I have this thing in my mouth." He sat forward and pointed to the back of his throat. "It's making me very uncomfortable, especially when I swallow."

He watched as her mind went through the possibilities. "Maybe you should see the dentist instead of the doctor."

"It's not my gums or teeth. I already thought about that," he responded in a deep voice full of frustration and longing.

"Okay." Alexis flipped open a steno pad, picked up a pen, jotting down some notes. "Excuse me," she said as her phone began to ring.

With an ease he recognized, she maneuvered the pen and paper to her left hand and began to scribble more things on the paper while she picked up the phone with her right. "HMC Rogets," came her greeting. "Yes, sir. I am in the middle of a consultation right now. Oh, yes, sir, he is the one in here. Just a moment, sir."

Alexis handed the phone across the desk. "Commander, it's for you." As soon as he took the phone, she turned around in her chair to give him privacy.

Frowning, Scott took the calm, a little annoyed they were being interrupted, but considering it was from his own superior officer, he tamped the emotion down.

"Sorry about that," he said a few moments later, handing her the phone.

"No prob," Alexis taking the phone from him as he lowered his large frame back into the chair. "Well, let me ask you some questions."

He just watched her, waiting, revealing nothing about what was going through his mind.

She shifted slightly in her seat and continued with her questions. "Are you taking any meds currently?"

He barely even blinked. "No."

"Fevers, sweats, or anything uncommon like that been happening?"

"No."

Her dark hand moved swiftly, taking down more notes. "How long have you felt this," pausing, Alexis narrowed her eyes and waved her hand, "this thing?"

"About five days now," he admitted, thinking back. That was the night of the gala in Hong Kong.

"All right..." She paused as a knock sounded on the door. "Yes?" It opened and in walked one of the corpsman with a few papers for her to sign. As she did, Alexis instructed the young man to make sure they weren't interrupted unless it was important. Since her eyes were looking at the papers, she missed the heated flare of desire in Scott's eyes.

The corpsman left quickly and soon it was back to the two of them in the small office. "Sorry, Commander, for the interruptions. Is there any chance you could have picked something up during your stay in Hong Kong?" Her voice was totally professional, as was her gaze.

"Nope." He leaned back again and held those unwavering eyes on hers. "And before you ask, not before that either. My last sexual encounter was..." He closed his eyes as if he had to remember.

He cracked open one eye and saw her clench her jaw as she waited for him to finish, giving off the appearance of being totally unaffected. He knew she definitely wasn't.

"Well, it was with someone who was clean. I know this for a fact," he stated as his eyes opened again to stare into her alluring ones.

"Very well then. As long as you are sure." More notes landed on the paper.

I am very sure, my gorgeous healer, for you were the last woman I was with. "I'm sure."

She cleared her throat dramatically. "Okay, have you been around anyone with strep that you know of? Or, actually, tell me where you were prior to Hong Kong; perhaps you got something there and it just took a bit of time to show symptoms."

His hand rubbed his throat and he cleared it a bit. "Everyone else in my team is fine. I am the only one feeling this way. It is leaving a bad taste in my throat. I don't even like the food that I normally eat."

"Okay, but remember, people don't react the same to being exposed to things; so while it may not have affected them, you might still feel the effects. As far as leaving a bad taste, I am not sure." She put down the pen and rose, walking over to a medical cabinet along a wall. "Let me just take a look and see if I can find anything."

Scott ran his eyes over the firm ass cupped by her khaki uniform. *God, I want to peel that off of her.* His body began to respond even more to her nearness; it was a miracle he hadn't taken her against the wall already, as randy as she was making him.

Alexis walked back over to him, hands gloved and holding a small penlight. "Tip your head back, Commander," she ordered.

Silent, he did as she bade and opened his mouth so she could peer into it. His eyes remained on her face when she leaned over him. He inhaled her soothing and yet damnably arousing feminine scent. He loved how she smelled. Like heather.

Finally, she stood up and clicked off the light. "I don't know. I don't see anything. There is no swelling, no redness. No indication of anything that could be irritated or infected." Her head tilted to the side as she thought about another cause and pulled off her gloves to toss them in the garbage.

Scott grabbed her wrist, halting her. At her look between his hand and his face, he said, "I know what it is."

His touch momentarily forgotten, her eyes flew up to meet his. "What is it?"

"My foot." He jerked his arm and she fell back across his lap, where he imprisoned her against his chiseled chest.

"Let me go!" she shrieked, struggling to get free.

"Ever since I said those horrible things to you in Hong Kong I have felt like this moronic asshole. I was jealous. I still am jealous," he muttered against her cheek where his lips were pressed.

"Let me go, Commander," she demanded even as he felt her body melt against him.

"Never, Lex, I can never let you go. I love you." His eyes closed as he nuzzled the smooth skin of her neck, once again feeling the completion this woman brought to his life.

She sank further into briefly before she froze. "Let me go! We are on the ship! Do you know how much trouble we would get into?" She struggled more.

His tongue trailed along her cheekbone. "No."

Alexis stopped fighting to get free; she was so shocked at his answer. "What do you mean, 'no'?"

"I'm not letting go of you until you hear me out." He kissed her neck.

She looked at him with wide eyes. "Someone could come in."

"Then I suggest you hold still and let me say what I want to say. We both know you can't get away from me."

"Why are you doing this to me?" She asked her panicked question in a hushed voice, as if the slightest noise would alert someone that she was on his lap.

"You told them you were in a consultation. The corpsman came in and saw that nothing was wrong. I don't know how you have been able to avoid me on this ship, but you have and I couldn't go another second without talking to you and trying to make up for my idiotic remark that I said in anger in Hong Kong." His fingers began to move up her bare arm. "Will you hear me out?"

"I don't have much choice, now do I?" She huffed, trying not to give in and lean against his body even more.

"I just want a chance to explain my actions," His body grew rigid as his tone lost all emotion, noticing her shift in posture. "If I offend you that much, maybe I should leave."

Putting her face directly into his, her eyes golden fire, she challenged him. "Maybe you should."

Eyes so blue they rivaled the sky narrowed, meeting her glare with his own. One blond eyebrow arched. "Fine." After being careful to make sure she stood securely on her feet, Scott stood abruptly. "Thanks for the advice, Chief." His chilling voice froze the entire room as his hand turned the knob on the door, opening it to allow their conversation to be overheard. "I understand now what you are saying."

"Good, Commander." She tilted up her proud chin, her expression set. "As long as it's clear. Have a good day, sir."

He watched her return to her computer, her back to him once more. Feeling more frustrated than ever, Scott left the room, shutting the door behind him.

Chapter Eighteen

Alexis willed the tears to not fall as she began to enter in more data into the computer. When she heard the door quietly close, her shoulders shuddered as she realized she'd just gotten rid of the best thing that would most likely ever happen to her. "*Jesú*, Alexis, you have to be the dumbest broad in the world! You know you love him. If you would just learn to control that temper and mouth of yours, you could've had the best man in creation around—to hold you, be with you and, most of all, love you," she muttered as her fingers typed in the information.

Alexis kept at it for about two more minutes before simply dropping her head forward to land on the smooth wood beside the keyboard. "I'm such an idiot," she wailed to the confines of the room. "I can't believe I let him go…"

"And I can't believe you actually thought I would let you go a second time, Alexis Milele Rogets." A velvet fold of seduction wrapped itself around her as those words were murmured into her ear.

Without raising her head, for fear it was just her imagination, she asked hesitantly, "Are you really here?"

Breath warmed her neck. "Turn your head and see for yourself."

Eyes that shone with unshed tears opened as her head turned. Alexis found herself looking into those beautiful, bedroom blue eyes. "I thought you left," she whispered, her mouth a hair's breadth away from his.

"I am not leaving you, Lex." Scott promised. His lips moved tenderly over hers as he spoke. "I'm so sorry for what I said to you in Hong Kong. I was being immature and jealous, can you forgive me?"

"I forgive you." *I want to kiss him so bad.*

"Do you have any idea how much I want to kiss you right now?"

"No," she breathed, hope plain in her eyes.

"I know we are on the ship and I would be breaking protocol," he said, offering her a chance to back out.

"I don't care. Kiss me, Scott," she ordered.

His eyes flashed. He didn't have to be told twice. With a slight movement of his head, he covered her lips with his firm ones. Kneeling beside her chair, he turned her body towards his, never breaking contact with her mouth.

Alexis brought her hands up to cradle his face, her dark skin contrasting beautifully with his tanned skin. The kiss was forgiving, gentle, and promised a future together. Her thick lashes fell to rest on her cheeks as she gave herself over to the sensation of being loved by this man.

He drew away from her slowly, pulling on her bottom lip and she felt his eyes waiting for hers to open again. "I have to stop or I am going to take this much farther."

She still didn't open her eyes. "Why didn't you leave like you said?"

"It is going to take a hell of a lot more than your temper to get me to leave your side, my amazing little healer." He caressed her full lips with his thumb. "I happen to like that spark in you."

Her exotic eyes widened. "So you heard me?"

"Yes, I heard. And I am waiting to hear it again." His eyes never relinquished their hold on her.

"I am in love with you, Lieutenant Commander Harrington Prescott Broderick Leighton the Third," she admitted, surprised at how easy it was to share that with him. Her fingers brushed tenderly over his temple. "I love you."

Eyes the blue of Gentian violets deepened with love and desire. "And I you, my stunning woman. And I you." His lips covered hers again, drawing them both closer to the point of no return.

As before, he was the one to draw away from her intoxicating lips, an act that got him a groan of frustration from her. "Now is not the time," he said, standing and moving back from her tempting body.

She grumbled her displeasure again but realized he was right. Her body was on full alert from his presence. The fact that he'd touched her only added fuel to the flames that coursed her body.

Alexis stood and moved towards him and the door. "Was there anything else you needed to discuss with me, Commander?" she wondered as she opened the door.

"I think that will take care of it. Again, thanks for seeing me," he said, brushing past her and his fingers grazing lightly along her ass, positive the act would be unobserved by the corpsman sitting out in the main area.

"That's what I'm here for," she responded, trembling from the contact.

Scott apparently heard the waver in her voice, for looked at her and winked, sending her a half smile. "Good to know. If the irritation comes back I will just come find you."

"Very good, Commander," Alexis said, her eyes drawn to his mouth as she unknowingly drew her lower lip into her mouth.

His eyes flared with desire. "I love you." He mouthed the words at her.

All she did was smile. And when he turned he found out why, there was a petty officer waiting to speak to her. "Good day, Commander." Alexis waved the petty officer into her office and, with only one quick glance at the man who held her heart; she went back to her job.

※

Walking into the exercise room, Scott stopped short, almost causing one of his teammates to run into him. Across the small room he saw Alexis on the treadmill, running and talking with the woman she had been with in Hong Kong. His gaze was frozen on her glistening body until Maverick, who was with him, shoved him in the shoulder, making him realize he was being rude and unprofessional.

As he went over to the weights, Scott watched her out of the corner of his eye. She wore a navy blue sports bra and a pair of running shorts with the word NAVY across the ass. Her hair was up in a ponytail and it swayed with every step she took.

"Man, at least sit down and pretend to be working out," Maverick whispered to him.

"What are you talking about?" Scott asked as he sat down on the Bowflex.

"The way you are staring at that stunning doctor. You need to stop before others pick up on it."

Scott's eyes flew to meet the dark ones of his teammate. "I wasn't—"

"Please, I am not that dumb. Just don't draw attention to yourself." Maverick sat down on the machine next to him.

They talked about things they planned to do when they made it back to the States. The pair easily answered some questions that other sailors had for them about being SEALs. And through it all, Scott kept watch on that NAVY across the finest ass he'd ever seen in his life.

When Alexis finally got off the treadmill and turned around, Scott got immense pleasure from watching her eyes darken as they moved over his body. Her face was partially covered by the towel she was using to mop the sweat off her brow but he knew her expressions. He nodded once at something someone near him said, even as his eyes ran boldly over her body.

"Damn, Lex," Katie said in Spanish. "Look at those men. And that blond one is looking over here. That's Commander Leighton. He's checking us out. Well, maybe it's you." Unabashedly Katie roved her eyes over the two SEALs exercising.

"I know who they are. I've met them before," Alexis responded in Spanish as she continued to blot away the sweat that seemed to be coming even more freely now that she was looking at Scott.

"Do you know what I would give for a night with them? Either one, I'm not picky," Katie asked as she joined Alexis on the mat to do their cool down.

Alexis snorted. "I can just imagine..." Closing her eyes, she tried to focus on calming her body down, not imagining what she *had* done with one of them for a few nights. And days.

"Oh, please, you can't tell me that you wouldn't want a go with either of them," Katie teased as they stretched.

I had a go. I had many "gos" with the blond one. "I didn't say that. All I said was I could imagine what you would give for a night with them." Refusing to open her eyes because she could feel Scott's blue eyes on her, Alexis continued to stretch.

"I am getting all hot and bothered just thinking about his hands on my body," came the breathless words.

"His?" Alexis asked.

"That blond one," Katie said.

Immediately Alexis's eyes flew open. It was all okay as long as she'd believed that Katie wanted Maverick; but the second Alexis found out it was Scott, she was beyond livid.

"I knew it," Katie gushed, still speaking in Spanish. "It was him." Her eyes pinned a look on Alexis that she knew she couldn't get out of. "He can't take his eyes off of you. And, you, I have never seen you stretch with your eyes shut."

"Katie," Alexis ground out. "Keep your voice down."

"Tell me I'm wrong," she challenged.

Meeting the dark gaze of her friend, Alexis shook her head. "I can't."

"Oh, my God," Katie squealed, only to immediately quiet down when people looked over at them. "We need to go talk. Now!" Tugging on Alexis's arm, Katie got them up and out of there before Alexis said another word.

"They seemed to be in a rush to leave," Maverick commented as he watched the two women head out the door.

I want to make love to her. "Guess so," Scott said between reps on the Bowflex.

"Like you didn't notice."

"Maverick," came the warning.

"Hey, at least with Tyson the warning came because he was married. What's your reasoning?" he prodded.

Scott cut his eyes over to his teammate. "She doesn't need to be a conquest. Don't even think about it, Maverick. You know what I did to my own brother." He let the threat hang.

"I do. But I am not saying anything bad about her." Black eyes glinted with trouble. "In fact, I would love to get to know her better."

"If you want to live to your next birthday, you will stay the fuck away from her," Scott growled.

"Tsk, tsk, tsk. If you injure me, I will just have to go to medical, now won't I?"

Taking a deep breath, Scott prayed for control. "Leave her alone, Maverick. She is mine."

"Well," Maverick said as he worked his legs even harder. "At least you are finally admitting it."

"Meaning?"

"You have been trying to avoid any and all talk of her since we found out you spent some down time with her at your cabin." Dark eyebrows rose and waited for the response.

"I wasn't sure what was going to happen. I'm still not," he admitted reluctantly.

"Man, first Tyson and now you. What is it with you? Both of you are men, Navy SEALs, and you are scared of a woman." Maverick shook his head.

"One day, Maverick, one day," Scott predicted as they climbed off the machines and headed towards the showers. "You are going to meet a woman who sends you spinning. All of your smooth lines and suave moves aren't gonna mean squat. The only thing that matters will be the way she looks at you, like you are her whole world. You will give up things and say things you never believed possible. And when that day comes, I will be right there to say, 'I told you so.'"

"There isn't a woman alive who can sucker me like that. I like being single."

Scott laughed. "So did I, until one day in Norfolk when my eyes fell upon the most beautiful woman I had ever seen. You know why I never went out with y'all after a mission? It was because of her. No other woman could even come close to how she made me feel."

"Jesus, man, you sound like a sap. You sound like Tyson," Maverick teased.

"I sound like a man in love. Just you wait, man. Your turn is coming."

"Hell, no," Maverick insisted and they entered the shower stalls.

An hour later, Scott was leaning on the barrier that kept him from tumbling down onto the lower deck. Below were Alexis and her friend who were staring out over the water watching the sun set. *I could stare at her all day, she is so beautiful.* He stood with Maverick, who was smoking a cigarette.

"You plan on burning a hole into her or are you going to talk to her?" Maverick's voice rang quietly in Scott's ear.

"I can't talk to her without just grabbing a hold of her. Damn it, Mav, when I saw her in her office all I wanted to do was take her against the wall. I don't have any control around her. And yet, at the same time, I can't stop watching her and I think I am going to do something that gets her into trouble. Maybe I should go stay on the *Endeavor*."

"Damn, man, you sound tore up about this." Maverick snubbed out his cigarette and faced his friend.

Scott dragged his stubborn gaze off the woman he loved more than he ever thought possible and placed it on his teammate. "James," he said using his friend's first name. "Never in my entire life have I ever felt this strongly about anyone. I don't know how to handle these feelings."

"Don't ask me, man. I just got finished telling you I love the single life. No, really, man. For what it's worth, I have never seen you seem that happy to just be in the presence of a woman." He smacked Scott on the shoulder. "She's good for you."

A grin crossed the blond SEAL's face, "You see that, too, huh? Over two years and I just now got her to tell me she loves me. I wanted to shout it to the whole world, but all I could do was kiss her quietly while a corpsman sat outside the door."

"Fraternizing on the ship..." Maverick tsked.

"Shut up, man. I don't know how this is going to work out, but I have to get her to accept it. This woman is like none I have ever met before."

Maverick held out his hands. "Please, stop with the praise train. I know you love her, but I don't want to hear every wonderful thing about *your* woman...unless you were planning on sharing..." One dark eyebrow rose.

With a harsh shout, Scott grabbed his friend around the neck. "You must have a death wish. I wouldn't share her for anything!"

"Okay, don't hurt me," Maverick teased as they disappeared into the grayness of the ship.

Chapter Nineteen

The fresh breeze off the Pacific flowed over Alexis. She smiled as water pelted her face. Tipping her head back, she allowed more to fall over her. She loved the rain, especially when she was on land.

She'd been home for two weeks now. The last time she'd seen Scott, Commander Leighton, was when they'd pulled into Hawaii. His team had disembarked there.

Alexis had managed to steal a few more kisses from him, but the risk was too much for her. So she had to settle for secret glances, winks, and caresses. It was all very cloak-and-dagger, and she'd loved every second of it, although she'd wanted nothing more than to have him make love to her in many different ways.

Now, she stood overlooking the ocean from the cliff and enjoying the downpour. "Well, I admitted I loved him, but that doesn't change anything between us."

"And why wouldn't it change anything, my sexy little healer?" That delicious voice wove through the raindrops to fall on her ears.

She spun around so fast she almost fell over, and his strong body was right there to hold her. "What are you doing here?!"

"Now, now, my love, don't you think I deserve a better welcome than 'what are you doing here?'" his voice teased.

Her eyes darkened with pleasure as she took a few steps back and eyed his attire. A snug black shirt and indecently tight jeans molded even closer with the rain, those, and a pair of hiking boots adorned his feet. Rivulets of water ran down his face as he stood there watching her with a sexy grin.

Alexis sucked her lower lip into her mouth as she walked towards him, the seductive sway of her hips clearly enchanting him given the way his eyes darkened. Dark hands slid up his wet shirt to hook behind his neck. Her eyes were sultry as she pulled his head towards her.

Her mouth brushed against his before her tongue traced his lips. Slipping between them, her tongue invaded his warmth. The first touch was electric. Shockwaves pulsated through both bodies as his arms slid around her back, drawing her in closer.

The skies opened up, sending down torrents of rain on the couple. It didn't matter; they continued to stand in each other's arms, lips locked and souls intertwined. Strong hands began to pull up her shirt. "Lex," he moaned into her mouth.

"How about this for a 'welcome'?" she purred as her hands went to work on his pants.

He drew back from her intoxicating mouth. "What are we doing?"

Looking up at him beneath the rain dripping down her face, she murmured, "Well, I know how long it has been for me, and know what I am doing, but maybe I wasn't good enough for you. Or whoever you were with last wasn't."

A wicked glint entered his gaze. "Oh, that last woman I was with left her mark on me. And trust me, she was *all* good." He regarded how her shirt molded to her body, her nipples visible against the fabric.

"Was she now?" Alexis quipped as her eyes narrowed.

"Most definitely." His hips bucked against her pelvis. "Would you like me to tell you what she did to me with whipped cream?"

She knew exactly what he was talking about. "It was me," she said.

"My beautiful little healer, you are all the woman I could ever need." His hands kept moving up, taking her shirt with it. Drawing it over her head, he dropped it on the ground, leaving her standing in her bra and jeans, rain sluicing down her toffee body.

With one quick motion he took off his own shirt and let it fall. Their hands caressed each other, the raindrops only adding to the sensation. Scott drew her back in for another lingering kiss. Her hand pulled down his zipper to slip one hand inside his soaked jeans and boxers, closing around his throbbing erection.

The cold raindrops seemed to add more steam surrounding the couple. Scott groaned as she began to stroke him, a slow steady motion obviously drove him crazy.

His hands moved to her jeans, unbuttoning them. Kneeling on the wet ground, he tugged the wet material down over her hips, down chocolaty smooth legs and off her feet.

From his position, he looked up. Her hair was slicked back from her face and her white bra and panties had become transparent thanks to the pouring rain. One hand moved up the outside of each leg until they reached the waistband of her underwear. Hands gripping each hip, he put his face at the apex of her thighs, the heat of his mouth contrasting the cold left by the rain.

"*Ohhhh*," she moaned as he breathed in her spicy scent. Her legs trembled and spread wider to support her better. Alexis shook even more as his tongue traced along the edge of her panties.

"You smell so good." His words vibrated against her, sending more impulses throughout her wanting body. "I wonder; do you taste as good as you smell?"

Scott trailed his fingers to the front of the waistband, his thumbs coming close to the velvet heat covered by the wet cotton. Then his hands retreated, leaving her frustrated.

Two quick jerks and her panties fell away, only to be swept away over the cliff by the wind. The couple didn't notice. His mouth closed over her and his tongue swept deep into her silken folds.

Alexis's head fell back and her hands pressed his head closer to her, encouraging him to continue. It didn't take her long to leave earth and head on to heaven.

Another scream ripped from her mouth and the wind and rain carried it away. Scott stayed where he was until her multiple orgasms stopped. He stood and pressed his lips to hers, his fingers slipping inside her wet body.

Alexis whimpered as he dominated her with his kiss. His fingers withdrew as they shared taste. One hand pressed against the back of her head, grinding their mouths closer yet. Her arms looped around his neck, not wanting to break the kiss.

Step by step, he walked them backwards. That hand dropped from her head to her waist, lifting her and pressing her back into the cold wet feel of a boulder. She felt him smile as she sucked in her breath from the cold intrusion. He lifted her a bit higher before setting her down, sliding his freed erection deep within her.

"*Jesú*," she moaned as she wrapped her brown legs around his waist to allow him deeper penetration. The rain increased and they heard the rumble of thunder.

Slowly he moved in and out of her wet heat. The boulder braced her back as his large, strong hands were on her full hips.

Dark eyes opened and met the blue ones of the man loving her. Alexis dropped her hands to rest on his muscled forearms, her nails digging in with every stroke he delivered to her.

Through the rain, Scott viewed the woman before him. How it looked to see water cascading down all over her brown skin. She thought it erotic to be dressed in nothing but a white bra that didn't conceal his view of her large, pebbled nipples.

The sight of his tanned hands gripping her sienna-hued hips as he drove into her, the view of her dark body opening to accept his lighter erection, turned her on even more…and apparently Scott as well, for he grew harder inside her and pumped faster.

It still wasn't enough. "Harder, Scott, harder." Alexis panted over the rain and increasing thunder.

The pounding surf below, the thunder above, and the steady rain that was all around, drowned out Scott's grunts. Her insides began tightening around him as his strokes came faster and harder.

"Scott!" Alexis shouted, the rain hitting her taut nipples and sending more tremors through her.

"Yes, baby. I'm right here." His thrusts came quicker.

"I'm going to come, Scott," she cried to the dark evening sky.

"Then come," he said. "Come for me, Lex," he ordered as he began to slam into her.

Alexis screamed, her head tipping back to face the full onslaught of the rain, nails digging into his flesh as she came with a vengeance.

The tight squeeze of her muscles around him drew Scott over the edge with her. He, too, yelled to the rainy sky as he came, buried as deep as he could be within her.

Knees wobbly, he withdrew from her, helped her to regain her own feet, before he sagged against the boulder. "Damn, woman, I think you are going to kill me." His arms brought her close for an eye-fluttering, soul-sucking kiss.

Suddenly exhausted, Alexis shuddered. "I'm cold."

He squeezed her closer and kissed her temple. "Let's get you clothed and out of this rain…"

Zipping up his pants, Scott took her hand and led them back to where he had removed their clothes. Alexis had her pants but her shirt and underwear were nowhere to be found.

"Where are the rest of my clothes? My shirt? Panties?" she asked, struggling to get her wet jeans back on.

With a shrug, he handed his wet, muddy shirt over to her. "Wear mine." The thunder cracked overhead. "I think it's time to get out of here."

Alexis agreed. Slipping his shirt on, she took his hand and grabbed her shoes with the other one. Holding hands, they ran back down towards the path that would lead them to the parking lot. One was dressed in jeans and boots, the other shoeless but wearing jeans and an oversized shirt.

They passed one couple on the trail who looked at them, grinning and yelling to their retreating backs, "Way to go!"

In the parking area, Alexis headed for her vehicle, unlocking it before they got there via keyless entry. Both of them jumped in and dripped all over her leather interior.

"I can't believe we just had sex in a public park," Alexis muttered and dropped her head against the steering wheel, still utterly mortified she'd been watched.

"We have never had sex, healer of my heart. It is so much deeper than that," he corrected and rubbed her back comfortingly.

"What else would you call rutting like animals against a rock in the rain?" she asked, finally sitting up and starting her vehicle. "With people watching."

"Fun as hell and better than cable," Scott teased.

"Scott..." she said, trying to sound indignant even though she laughed internally.

"Yes, my gorgeous healer?" Reaching across the vehicle, he brought them closer for a kiss.

"I can't remember," she claimed as he pulled away.

"Good." Scott kissed her again. This time, his hand tried moving underneath the shirt she wore. "My clothes look so good on you."

"No." She drew, back pushing his hand away. "Where is your car?"

"On the East Coast."

Her eyes narrowed. "How'd you get here?"

"Taxi."

"What are you doing here? Where are you staying, for that matter?"

"With you," he responded immediately.

Alexis snorted. "Of course you are. You don't have a clue where I am staying but you are staying with me."

"You are staying at your brother's condo. Piers, the one you were with in Hong Kong. Like you do every time you are in port here," Scott replied.

Why am I not surprised he knows this? "And you assumed you would be welcome?"

"Four days, Lex." He paused. "And you know you aren't surprised because I don't want to make a mistake like I did before, by jumping to the wrong conclusion."

What is he doing, reading my mind now? "Four days what?" She began to drive.

"No, I can't read your mind, but your thoughts are all over your face. And you owe me four days. Or are you going back on your word?"

"So what, you gonna be my weekend lover?" she questioned as they got on the interstate.

He didn't answer that, though his expression told her he didn't appreciate the insinuation. "Go to dinner with me tonight. A nice dinner."

"And what will you wear?" Alexis asked with a pointed look at his shirtless body.

He arched an eyebrow at her. "I have other clothes, you know."

"I'm sure you do."

"So, is it a date?" They pulled into a nice condo community.

Like I am going to turn down spending time with you! "Sure. You can come in, get dry, and I can take you to wherever you're staying."

"I already told you where I was staying."

"Right, right," she muttered, pulling into a two car garage. "With me."

"Exactly." He got out and waited for her to come around the front of the vehicle.

Together they walked through the door and into the mud room. Grabbing towels, she threw one at him. "This will work until we get robes. Just leave your wet clothes here. I'll wash them later."

With an easy shrug, he began to disrobe. Alexis was frozen as she watched him remove his boots, socks, pants — and, finally — boxers. Every muscle rippled as he moved. She barely managed to contain her groan of disappointment when the dark gray towel was secured around his lean waist.

"Keep looking at me like that and I will take you on the floor in here," Scott said, pulling her eyes up from his crotch to meet his gaze.

"Sorry," she mumbled even as her body grew wet at the image.

"Never apologize for wanting me. Aren't you disrobing? It's only fair I get to watch you now." He leaned against the wall, defined arms crossed over his naked, muscular torso.

Alexis met his gaze and jerked his shirt off over her head. Then, as his blue eyes darkened with desire, she removed her bra. Sliding her jeans down, she kicked them away and reached for the towel Scott held out to her.

Her hand touched the thick cotton but when she pulled, she was met with resistance. Alexis found herself being reeled in towards the golden god who stood in the room wearing nothing but a towel.

"Arms up," came his soft order when her body halted between his legs. Wordlessly she complied, keeping her swirling gaze on his face.

Taking the towel, Scott opened it behind her. His gaze took in the full breasts that still had puckered nipples, the flare of her curvaceous hips, her flat belly. He licked his lips as his eyes moved over the nicely trimmed patch of black hair between her legs and down her strong legs to the bright pink on her toenails.

Moving his eyes leisurely back up her body, he wrapped her sensual figure in the thick towel and tucked the end in over her breasts so it would stay put. "It seems to me, my sexy healer, that is one lucky towel to be touching that exquisite body of yours." His lips brushed hers before he enfolded her into his embrace.

Alexis sighed contentedly and pressed her cheek against his marbled chest, letting the rhythmic beating of his heart flow through her.

Chapter Twenty

"*Mmmm*, what a way to spend a weekend," Scott murmured in his deep timbre.

Alexis's hand ran idly up and down his chest and her head was nestled against his shoulder. It was afternoon on Sunday, and they'd spent the past day and a half making love. The only time they left the bed was to get some food, and even those trips usually turned into a whole other experience of learning about one another's body.

A smile, one of total gratification and ease, crossed Alexis's face. They'd just been cuddling in the large bed for the past three hours talking about odd subjects and dozing, just happy to be with one another.

"I agree," she said in a hushed voice. The light sounds of romantic jazz played throughout the room.

"What are we going to do today?" His lips nuzzled her forehead. "What is left of today, I should say."

"Well, I have to get ready to go back to the ship. Can I take you somewhere?"

"My lovely little healer, you have taken me to just the place I want to be." His hands moved in slow circles around her silken skin.

"I mean to wherever you need to be." Her arm slid around his waist as she tucked herself closer yet.

I am right where I need to be. "When will you get another vacation?" he asked.

"Not for a while, I'm sure. Why?"

"I want you to come back and see me. Stay at the cabin with me." *Marry me.*

Eyes closed, Alexis smiled wider. "I can't just go across the country. I am stationed out here."

"I know, I know. Trust me, I know that." He groaned. "That is a problem."

"What are you talking about? I like the West Coast."

"And I like the East Coast, but something is missing."

"What would that be, Mister SEAL Man?" Her fingers moved across his ribs.

"You," he said directly. "You know how I feel about you, Alexis."

Sitting up, she cut him off before he could say another word. "Please don't. Don't say something that we will regret later. Just enjoy right now."

His eyes narrowed but he clamped his mouth shut. *What are you running from, Alexis? I know you love me, you told me so. Why are you so hesitant about there actually being an "us" for longer than a few days?* He pulled her back down across his chest, placing them nose to nose. "Well, there is something that we could do that I would enjoy. I believe there is a bit more of that chocolate sauce and edible strawberry oil." Scott rolled them over so Alexis was beneath him.

※

The booth was dark, private, and intimate. The single flame flickering between Scott and Alexis did nothing more than cast a gentle glow over their features. Empty plates were scattered across the table as they shared one piece of a five-layer chocolate cake, Scott feeding her and himself.

They sat on the same side. Alexis had her feet curled up under her and one hand on the inner thigh of the man beside her. They were relaxed, comfortable, and in love.

The waiters watched from a distance, rarely going over to interrupt them. The couple never raised their voices, choosing instead to whisper to one another. The man was constantly touching her face, brushing her hair back, or tracing her jaw line.

"What does your brother Piers do?" Scott asked as he slid a forkful of the decadent confection into his mouth.

"Piers is a diplomat, which would explain why he was over in Hong Kong. I am not entirely sure exactly what he does; all I know is he is important to the President and does tons of traveling." Her index finger wiped off the extra frosting at the corner of his mouth and sucked it clean herself.

Feeling himself stir as he watched her draw her finger into her mouth, Scott gulped hard. "And your other siblings?"

"The other ones…let me see." She paused for a bite of cake, smiling in ecstasy as its moistness covered her tongue. Swallowing, she picked up her cup of hot water and lemon to wash down the bite.

"Well?" Scott prompted, eating another forkful of cake.

"Well, Maurice is the oldest. He is an orthopedic specialist. He lives in Manhattan, married to a very nice woman, Lyn. She is an interior designer and they have four kids. Piers is next in line and, well, you know about him. Then there is—"

"Kieran, the one who called when you were at my place," Scott interrupted.

"Exactly. Kieran is a private investigator. Not married and he has one son." She rested her head on his shoulder. "Then there is Gamaliel, last I heard about him was he was over in Africa somewhere sticking his nose in places it shouldn't necessarily be. He's a missionary."

"Why do you say it like that? Missionaries are important."

"Yes, as long as they don't force their personal beliefs on another culture so much they lose where they came from. I just think my brother is a bit over the top sometimes." A wry smile crossed her face. "We all went into a profession, or calling according to Gamaliel, to help someone."

"I bet your family get-togethers are loads of fun."

"I haven't been to one in a few years. But the ones I remember, yes…tons of fun."

"Where does Jay fit into all this?" Scott set down the fork, for the cake was gone.

Alexis released a short bark of laughter. "Jay." Scott wasn't quite sure what that laugh meant. "Well, Jay…Jay is like a third cousin, but he has always been a troublemaker. I don't know the whole story, but we have an understanding between us. He is always welcome to stay at my house as long as he treats me and my things with respect."

The young doctor readjusted herself on the booth, putting her legs across his lap and watching him. "Tell me about your family," she prompted with a frown as she noticed the empty plate. The frown smoothed out when his hand began to caress the inside of her calf.

"Let me see, you already met Reeve. He is next in line after me. Nothing more than a playboy. Godric is next and he is the owner of one of the country clubs down there." Scott turned his gaze to meet Alexis's in the soft light. "The baby in the family is our sister, Corliss. She is in medical school."

"Good for her." Alexis stretched. "Well, now that *you* have eaten all the cake, let's go."

"I ate? Me?" he huffed. "I know you ate most of it."

"You had the fork, buddy, not me."

He waved the waiter over. "Check, please." His blue eyes moved over the woman next to him, an action that brought a smile to his face. Scott never believed how much enjoyment he derived just by being in her presence.

After paying he slid his wallet back into his jeans, then he slipped out of the booth, waiting for Alexis to do the same. He escorted her through the restaurant, his strong hand resting on the small of her back. Many stares followed them as they maneuvered through the tables. None of their audience seemed to wish them ill or challenge the man who carried himself with such authority.

"Let's go to a movie," Alexis suggested as they reached her newly cleaned Expedition.

"Sure. I'm game." A smile appeared on his features as he pictured her mood after a romantic movie. Although he couldn't claim to be fond of them, Scott was willing to sit through a "date" movie just for her.

"Great." Alexis slid her arm through his as they left her vehicle where it was and headed towards the multiplex at the other end of the mall.

Stopping in front of the sign, they both scanned the featured titles. Glancing up at the handsome man beside her, Alexis waited for him to say something.

"What do you think, Lex?" he asked, pulling her to rest against his chest, unaware of the envious looks other women were sending her.

"You tell me."

"No." His chin came to rest on the top of her head. "Ladies' choice."

Casting her eyes back towards him she wondered, "Does that hold up for later as well?"

"Anytime, anyplace," he responded, pinching her ass.

"*Ohhh.* Stop teasing." One manicured finger pointed at a new vampire movie. "How about that one?"

I'm impressed. "Are you sure?"

If her head hadn't been underneath his chin, his jaw would have dropped open at the sound of her "bloodlust". "Hell, yeah! 'Posed to be lots of blood, explosions, you know…good movie stuff!"

"I take it you don't go in for the fluffy movies?" Scott asked as he steered them into the line for tickets.

She grinned at him. "Wouldn't be my first choice. I like my gore."

"And the surprises keep on coming," he said, getting their tickets and then going in line for snacks.

"What? You thought I would like romantic movies, all the heartfelt goo?"

"Well, yes, I did. I mean, that *is* what most women like."

She laughed as she moved up another place in line. "And just when did you think I was like most women?"

His eyes raked over her backside. "Never, which is why I love you." Scott picked her up from behind and growled into her neck.

She squealed. "Put me down, Commander!"

He did so, albeit reluctantly. "What do you want?"

"Nachos, chocolate, popcorn, and a drink."

"Damn, didn't I just feed you?" he questioned lightheartedly, before relaying her order to the concession person. "What kind of chocolate?"

"Junior Mints and those Nestle Bites," she said, smirking. "That'll teach you to eat all a woman's cake."

"Would you like a pickle with this?" Scott teased.

"Why would I…? Oh, shut up." Her hand snaked out to hit him in the arm, but instead, she found herself pressed up against his broad chest.

"Ever hopeful." He kissed her quickly before turning his attention back to the pimple-faced kid behind the counter.

Loaded with their snacks, Scott and Alexis walked to the theater where their movie was showing. Climbing up to the back, they sat down. "Sure you don't want to be closer?" Scott asked. "Not that being in the back wouldn't have its benefits."

"I don't like people behind me." Her response was so fast he knew she wasn't being coy.

"Understood." He placed their spread of food out so she would have easy access to it all and they played the trivia game that was scrolling across the screen.

Alexis had answered the last question right and was one ahead when the lights dimmed and the previews began. The movie was horribly gory and great fun, right up both of their alleys.

When the lights turned up after the movie ended, Scott and his darkly gorgeous date stayed in their seats waiting patiently for the crowd to thin out. Finally, they rose and walked slowly down the steps and, after a stop at the trash, they headed out into the night.

"Thank you for such a wonderful evening, Lex," the deep voice said as they moved easily together across the near empty parking lot.

"Thank you. I had a really good time." She nudged him as they approached her vehicle.

"Me too." His sincere response came immediately.

※

Alexis's eyes opened slowly at the tender caress on her forehead. The low light from the bedside table was on, showing her the blond man who looked down upon her. Scott was sitting beside her and his hand was amorous as it moved her loose hair away from her face.

"What time is it?" she asked in a raspy voice.

"Early," he said in a hushed voice. "Go back to sleep."

They had made love upon their return from dinner and the movie to finally fall asleep around two in the morning. What did he consider early? She was getting up at five. "What's the time?"

"Three-thirty," Scott said.

"So what are you doing dressed?"

"My beeper went off. I have to go." He put those damnably gorgeous eyes on her. Immediately wide awake, Alexis got up so she could get out of bed. "What are you doing?" he asked, pressing her back down into the mattress.

"Don't you need a ride?"

"I called a taxi. You get some more sleep." His firm lips found her full, soft ones. "I just wanted to watch you sleep for a bit."

"I can take you," Alexis protested, feeling tears form in her eyes. Now she was beginning to know how spouses felt when they sent their sailors off to sea.

"No, my sexy healer. You stay here, sleep, and get to work on time." Scott stretched out beside her so they were face to face. "Don't forget about me."

Trying for a smile, Alexis shook her head. "I won't. Stay safe?" She meant it as a statement but it came out as a question.

"I will do my damnedest. I love you, Lex."

"I love you, too, Scott." Her hands moved to cup his face as she put their mouths together.

One more fast, hard kiss and he stood, gathered his sea bag, and saluted her before disappearing out the bedroom door. Alexis closed her eyes and willed the tears not to fall when she heard steps in the hallway. Scott had come back. "One more kiss," he groaned as he placed his lips on hers once more. "Love you," he yelled as he headed back up the hall.

"I love you, too," Alexis mumbled as she snuggled back down into the mattress, cuddling the pillow that still smelled of Scott to her face and succumbed to tears and sleep.

Chapter Twenty-One

USS Everett

"So, I know that I am going to regret losing you, but who can argue with SecNav?" Commander Touchette said to the woman who sat across from him at his desk.

"I understand, sir. I'll be ready to go in no time," the flat response came.

"Speak freely, Chief. I *am* sorry to lose you."

A smile crossed the beautiful face. "And I'm sorry to go. Did they say why me?"

Touchette shook his head. "Not that they felt the need to share with me. Just that they were sending your replacement out and we are to send you back on the same COD."

Alexis did her best to hide a grimace. The Carrier Onboard Delivery plane. *Nothing like catching a ride on that!* Being catapulted off the deck wasn't exactly fun in her opinion. "It has been an honor and a pleasure to serve under you, sir," she said, standing and offering her hand out to the older man.

"The pleasure is all mine. Now, go get packed. We will helo you over to the carrier in thirty. Dismissed."

Snapping to attention, she nodded and spun on her heel to head back to her rack and pack her belongings. *This is one weird tour.*

She reached women's berthing and gathered her belongings. Alexis was just about done when she heard a knock on her door. "Come in…"

"I can't believe you are leaving!" The whine came from behind her.

Alexis smiled sadly, tying up her sea bag. "Me, either. I liked being out here."

Katie approached, a forlorn look upon her face. "We will stay in touch, right?"

"Of course we will, Katie." A smile crossed Alexis's face as she hugged her friend. "Friends for life," she said in Spanish as she shouldered her sea bag and garment bag and headed towards the ladders to get to the helo pad.

Virginia

"We have temporary housing set for you, ma'am, until you figure out what you want to do," the seaman said as she took one of her bags and led the way.

Temp housing? Well, I should be happy it is bigger than my space on the ship. "Thank you, seaman," Alexis said as she followed the young woman up the steps and into her transitory home.

"After you get settled, ma'am, a car will be ready to take you to the hospital. Admiral Larkin is expecting you."

A freakin' admiral? Great, now I really have to watch my mouth! "I will be back down in ten minutes," Alexis said as she looked around her small room. *Time to find a place to rent.*

Stowing her gear swiftly, Alexis did a quick once-over of her uniform. She was exhausted but she still had to go check in before she could commit to some much-needed shuteye. Pulling her hair back into a new, tighter bun, she went back down to the early July afternoon, putting on her cover, her hat, as soon as she got outside. The car was waiting as promised and soon Alexis was being taken to Norfolk to check in with her new commanding officer, Admiral Larkin.

※

Not the best day but at least it is over. Alexis shut the door to her weeks' old apartment as she dropped her things on the polished hardwood floors and then ran to the sink for a glass of cold water. It had been one emergency after another today and she was exhausted.

"God, I hate this heat!" she swore, draining the glass in one gulp. Running water over her hand, Alexis applied it to the back of her neck, trying to cool herself down. She'd been here for two weeks now, and she could say without a doubt summer in Virginia was not pleasant.

As the cool air of her dwelling finally sank in, she walked back to her bags to put them in their proper place. Standing in her kitchen as she made herself a salad, Alexis was listening to an R&B mix when her cell phone began to chime.

"What if it is them calling me back? I need some rest," she moaned, hesitating to pick up the phone. *Too bad I can't just ignore it.* Flipping it open, she answered, "Rogets."

"Hello, sexy," the baritone voice caressed her through the phone.

Tears formed in her eyes. Biting back a smile she answered, "Hey, yourself, handsome." It had been almost two months since he'd left her sleeping in bed.

"You know who this is, right?"

"Isn't this the Marine that I met two nights ago at the bar?" she teased.

The growl was fully audible to her. "Lex."

She began to laugh. "How are you, Commander?"

"Good. We just landed today. Happy birthday."

"You remembered!" Alexis smiled as the tears began to fall.

"Of course. Didn't you get the flowers I sent?" he asked.

"No, but I'm not with the *Everett* anymore," she began as a knock came on her door. "Just a sec, someone is at the door."

"Okay."

Alexis walked over to the door and opened it to admit a man holding a huge bouquet of mixed flowers. "Thank you, just a sec and I will get you a tip."

The delivery man shook his head. "It's been taken care of. I have one more; I will be right back."

"Okay, the door will be open, just come on in." Alexis walked back to the phone and picked it back up. "You are the sweetest man around."

Scott said, "I know. Did you like the roses?"

Narrowing her eyes, she reached for the card that was in the bouquet. All it said was, *For the love of my life.*

"Well? Did you?" Scott asked again.

"I am looking at a mixed bouquet."

"Well, I sent roses." There was a hint of anger in his voice.

"He said he had another delivery for me," Alexis tried.

"Who else is sending you flowers?"

"I don't know. The card isn't signed," she said. Another knock on the door and Alexis yelled, "Come on in. Just set them down and I will sign for them in a moment."

"Who else is sending you flowers?" The question was repeated, but it was coming from behind her.

Confused, Alexis turned and came face to face with the man she had missed so much. "Scott!" she squealed, dropping the phone and running over to him as he set down the two dozen blood-red roses on her table and jumping into his arms. He caught her around the waist.

Their lips met hungrily. Alexis had her legs and arms around him as she removed her lips from his. "What are you doing here? Why are you here? And, for that matter, how did you know where to find me?"

"I will always know where to find you, Lex." His words made her feel so safe. "And I'm here because I missed you."

"I missed you too." They were nose to nose.

"I would love to show how much I missed you, but I have to get to Norfolk. I have an appointment with JAG."

Her face fell as her legs unhooked from his body. "Okay. Thanks for the flowers, and for stopping in."

"I have to go now or," he paused and his eyes boldly moved up and down her body. "Or I won't make my appointment, my enchanting healer." He kissed her again and stepped away from her to caress her lips with his thumb. His eyes were gentle as they looked upon her face.

"Bye, Commander." Alexis said, trailing two fingers down his tee shirt.

"Until later, my love." With a wink he was gone, leaving her alone—alone with the flowers and unfilled desires.

It was close to midnight when Alexis padded towards her bedroom. The weather just felt too sticky to sleep so she stayed up reading the latest medical thriller she had purchased at the grocery store. Since it was her birthday and the weekend, staying up late wasn't a bad thing. The doorbell rang while she was in the process of removing her tank top. Pulling it back down, she walked into the living room and opened the door.

"What the hell are you doing opening the door this time of the night without asking who it is first?" demanded the man on the other side.

With a shrug, Alexis slammed the door closed in the man's face. "Suit yourself," she muttered. Arms crossed, she remained there waiting for the inevitable.

The man on the other end didn't disappoint. "Lex!" he thundered. "Open this here door!"

Leaning her back against the cool wood her voice rang out sugary sweet. "Who is it?"

"Alexis," the masculine voice dropped further.

"I'm sorry. I don't know any men named Alexis." She tried not to laugh at the words coming out of that man's mouth. "Do you kiss your mother with that mouth?" she admonished through the door.

"I'll kiss you with it if you'd open the damn door," he growled.

"Tsk, tsk, tsk. I don't want any potty mouth near me." Alexis laughed, swinging the door open and hugging the man who stood there.

"Good to see you, Lex," he said affectionately, kissing her on the cheek.

"And you. Come on in. What are you doing here?" Alexis drew the man into her apartment as he reached behind him to grab his suitcase. Her eyes traveled fondly over the tall, muscular black man.

"Convention. Figured I'd stay with you." He hugged her again. "That okay by you?"

"Fine by me." Leading the way, she walked to the guest room. "How is Sean?"

"Well," the man said in his low voice. "He's a teenage boy. He's with his mother's parents. Wanted to come with me, but they asked to keep him a while." Opening a suitcase, the man pulled out a wrapped box. "For you."

"What is it?"

"Just open it," he answered with a shake of his dark head.

Alexis sat down on the edge of the bed and opened the small box. Inside was a ring box, light gray in color. Opening that, her mouth fell open as she looked at the ring perched inside.

It displayed a platinum band inlaid with peridot and tanzanite. She loved its simple elegance from the moment her eyes lay upon it. "Ohhh," Alexis breathed, almost hesitant almost to touch it.

Kneeling before her he took the ring out of the box. "Go on, it's for you. Happy birthday, darlin'."

Alexis sipped it on over her ring finger on her right hand. A perfect fit. "I have always wanted this ring." Her expressive eyes met his and a brilliant smile lit up her face. "Why would you do this?"

"Yes. Why would you do that?" A new voice entered the conversation, drawing up two pairs of stunned eyes.

Reacting quickly, the man who'd been kneeling jumped up at the man standing in the doorway wearing a scowl on his face. The altercation was over before it really even began.

"Scott, no!" Alexis shrieked as he held the man who attacked him immobile. "Let him go!" She jumped up and inserted her body between the two men.

Seductive blue eyes were hard with rage as he followed the Alexis's bidding. His body stayed alert to the motions of the other man rubbing his arm and sending him evil looks. "Who is he, Lex? And why was he on his knees giving you a ring?" The anger-laden tone filled the small room.

One hand on Scott, Alexis reached out toward the other man only to find herself hauled up against one very pissed off SEAL. "This is my brother Kieran, Scott. My brother. The ring is a birthday present." Her eyes rose up and met his, begging him to understand. "Kieran, are you okay?"

"Sis, tell me right now why some white man just walked into your apartment and froze my movements like nobody's business."

Electing to stay up against Scott's chest but turning to face her brother, Alexis began to talk. "This is Scott, he's my...my...my...." Her face scrunched up as she lost any idea of what she was going to say. How did she classify her relationship with Scott? She knew what she wished it to be, but not how he classified it.

"Her man," the arrogant SEAL inserted.

Kieran's dark eyes grew wide. "Her man? You are *her* man? You?"

"Yep," Scott answered without missing a beat.

Pinning his eyes on his youngest sibling, Kieran was shocked. "Sis?" He asked the question about the truth of Scott's statement without verbalizing it.

Not looking back at the man whose chest she leaned on, she stuttered, "Well, we are kinda together."

"Kinda?" Her brother sounded skeptical.

"Kinda?" Scott sounded pissed, and he spun her around so he could look at her.

Scott felt his heart clench all over again. It'd happened earlier when he'd come back to Alexis's apartment after having dinner with some friends to see her door ajar. He'd gone completely into battle mode, moving swiftly and silently throughout the dwelling, promising excruciating harm should someone have hurt her. The sight of a man kneeling before her and presenting her with a ring hadn't lessened his urge to fight; in fact, it had increased it. The only reason the man still breathed was because he was Alexis's brother.

But that feeling compared to what he experienced now.

He watched as Alexis realized how furious and hurt he was. Ignoring her brother, she instead focused on him. "Well, we never really defined our relationship."

His eyes narrowed. *What the hell kind of shit is this?* "We're sleeping together. To me, that's pretty damn defined." Scott blinked slowly several times, unbelieving she could think this was a fling.

"I didn't want to make any assumptions about how you felt," Alexis mumbled, dropping her eyes.

"So you were okay with just being a booty call for me?" His tone lowered dangerously as it turned sarcastic.

Her eyes flew to his. "Don't take that tone with me!" She stepped back. "You know, just as I do, we are break—"

"Breaking the rules. I know. I get that," he snapped, cutting her off. "Jesus, Alexis, can you ever get past that?" Scott shoved his fingers through his short hair. "We don't serve together and there is no way you would ever be working with me."

Those tiger eyes narrowed with building rage. "No way? And why would that be? Because you are nothing more than an arrogant, egotistical man who happens to be a Navy SEAL? And I am nothing more than a mere woman?"

"That isn't what I meant," he growled.

"Then what? Why would I never be working with you? Not smart enough? Tall enough? *White* enough?" Alexis moved away from him and took refuge beside her silent brother who stood watching this interaction with amusement. "Maybe you should leave," she told Scott.

Disappointment was plain as he shook his head. "I think you're right. I guess I was wrong when I thought we had gotten past this whole color thing. I never lied to you, Alexis. I meant everything I said, especially the part about being too old to play games."

Scott shrugged as he fought to get the next words out. "When you are done with these foolish thoughts and believe you are ready for a real relationship with a *man*, not a boy, let me know."

However, mere seconds passed and Alexis was in his arms again. "I know I'm arrogant, but we both know I am the *only* man who can make you feel complete." His lips possessed hers for a moment before he released her and said to her sagging body, "Goodbye, my healer." He was gone.

Chapter Twenty-Two

Groaning, Alexis pushed up from her kneeling position in front of the toilet. "I feel like shit," she moaned to the room as she washed her mouth out again and flushed the handle on the porcelain god she had just spent the past few hours worshipping.

She stumbled back into her bed and collapsed. It had been two weeks since Scott had left her place. No calls, no visits, nothing but an endless supply of memories. "Okay, I get it. I was wrong for jumping to conclusions," Alexis yelled to the empty room. As the thought of never seeing him again crossed her mind, another wave of nausea swept her.

Despite the hot summer night, she curled up under the thick down comforter. Eyes closed, she felt her body finally begin to relax. *Good, I need some sleep.* She could see Scott in her mind, reaching out for her, beckoning to her. His face was full of forgiveness for her stupidity, yet just as their fingers were about to touch....

The sound of her pager vibrating on the bedside table along with the loud ring from her cell phone jerked her back awake. *Both? Why the hell would they both be going off?*

Her eyes opened reluctantly. *Wow, I must have gotten some sleep after all.* It was dark. Picking up the pager, she turned on the light by her bed and looked at the number just as her phone began to trill again.

The hospital.

Alexis responded immediately. Adrenaline raced to every part of her body as she dressed in record time, stopping only to grab her purse and keys before her shoed feet were running her swiftly down the hall of the building and out the door to her vehicle.

Eighteen hours later an extremely exhausted Alexis groaned as she sipped her bottled water. There were times that working in a military hospital was worse than being in residency. This was one of those times.

"You okay, Lex?" another doctor Sharon asked as she stopped by, grabbing a seat in the break room.

"Just wiped. I wasn't feeling the best when the call came in to get here," Alexis answered, rolling her shoulders to get the tension out. It didn't work.

Sharon looked on with concern. "You haven't been yourself for a few weeks now. Is everything okay?"

"Fine. Just still getting settled in. Thanks for asking." *Sure I'm fine, why wouldn't I be? I chased off the best man in the world!*

"Well, let me know if there is anything I can do to help you out."

"Thanks, Sharon, I appreciate that." Alexis stood and swallowed to keep the bile down. "I have to get some shut eye." With a wave over her shoulder, Alexis left the room and soon the hospital.

※

"What?" Alexis screeched. "That can't be! Run it again!"

Sharon just looked at her. "I know what I'm doing, Lex. Those are the results."

"We need to do another blood draw just to be sure," Alexis protested, walking towards a new syringe pack.

"No, we don't." The pale hand grabbed hold of Alexis and stopped her. "We checked, double-checked, and checked again. These are the results, and getting more blood isn't going to change that fact." Sharon's green eyes were honest and straightforward as she made sure to meet Alexis's gaze.

"Aww, shit. I know you're right. I just…" Alexis trailed off as she sat down on the black stool and rubbed her face. *What else can go wrong for me?*

Closing the door, Sharon grabbed another stool and pulled it close to Alexis and sat down so they were knee to knee. "Look, Lex, I know we haven't known each other for very long but I do consider you a friend. A good friend. And since I know I am a good friend," she quipped playfully. "I am going to be nosy."

Alexis smiled at her friend. "Go on and be nosy then."

"Were we not pleased with the news?"

Pleased? Pleased? More like shocked. "I'm not sure how I feel yet. Except amazed."

Sharon raised a plucked eyebrow. "Didn't they explain to you how this happened?"

Despite the seriousness of the situation, a laugh erupted out of Alexis. "I think I heard something about it along the way."

"What are you going to do?"

Therein, my dear friend, lies the question. What am *I going to do?* "I don't know, Sharon. I don't know."

"He deserves to be told," Sharon's smooth voice said.

"I know. I'll do it," she said solemnly, looking at the door like there would be some big thing to stop her from having to deliver the news.

"Will you be okay? Do you want me to go with you?"

"No!" Alexis touched her friend's arm. "I didn't mean to snap. I just think that it would be best for me to do this alone."

"Well, you know how to find me. Call me, page me, or just yell really, really loudly, until I hear you," Sharon said with a small smile. "I'll see you in twenty-four." Then the blonde woman was gone. A few minutes passed before Alexis left the examination room to do rounds, her mind still reeling from what she'd just learned.

Hours later, a very solemn Alexis walked into her apartment. Her body was on autopilot as she went through her normal routine. Listening to her messages, she got herself a small bite to eat. There was nothing from her machine that needed to be attended to right now.

Stomach feeling a bit better, Alexis took a shower. Her body clean, relaxed, and dressed in a simple white silk two-piece sleepwear set, she washed her dishes and straightened up her apartment. As she cleaned, she noticed the light flashing on her machine again. So, after pressing the "play" button, she listened as she refolded the blanket to go over the back of her couch. It was from the admiral. He wanted her at his office before she reported for duty. *Jesus, this man is a pain in my ass.* Jotting the information down where she would remember it, she re-secured the lock on her door and went to bed.

※

Nodding at the couple in the elevator, Alexis slipped into the back and rested against the cool panel. Two more people entered as the door shut, but Alexis just kept her eyes closed. She didn't want to invite conversation.

Getting off on the fifth floor, Alexis smiled at the four people as she got off. A real smile found its way onto her face when she saw Sharon waiting for her. "Morn', Sharon. How are you?"

"We are on the way to see the admiral, how do you think I am doing?" she responded with a smile.

"Yeah, I wonder what we did this time." They fell instep with one another.

Walking around the corner, a high feminine laugh reached them. Both women looked at one another and just shook their heads. It was a laugh that shouldn't be allowed in public. The grating sound came again as they headed around the last corner before they reached the corridor that housed the admiral's office.

Alexis almost tripped over her feet. There, leaning against the corner, stood Lieutenant Commander Leighton laughing and talking to a tall, leggy blonde woman. *Didn't take him long to get over me.* Biting the inside of her lip to keep her face emotionless, she focused straight ahead and kept walking.

Scott felt Alexis before he saw her. He was standing in the hallway with a woman who had been glued to him for the past two weeks. Every time he showed up here, she followed him around. He believed her name was Lisa, but he couldn't for the life of him recall that with any certainty.

He knew he laughed politely at her joke, but everything else fled his mind except for the all-consuming passion he felt for a woman he hadn't seen for a few weeks. Scott didn't know the woman who walked beside her, but he didn't care. He only cared about Alexis.

Hell, he missed her. Hotheaded and full of male arrogance, he had walked out on the best thing he'd ever had. Being in the same town with her and not seeing her was killing him. Going to the hospital just to lay his eyes on her radiant beauty was a frequent thought in his mind.

Now that he was here, Scott couldn't believe his bad luck. He finally gets to see Alexis and this "Lisa" character was occupying his attention. Knowing Alexis saw him standing there, he grew stony as he felt her slight. He could demand she acknowledge him, but the last thing he needed to do was reinforce the difference in their ranks.

Intense blue eyes followed Alexis and her friend's progress down the hall until they knocked and entered into a room. "What are you staring at, Commander? Or should I say whom?" The abrasive blonde's voice reached his ears.

"Huh?" He blinked and had to struggle to focus back on Lisa. "I thought I saw someone that I worked with a while ago. Sorry, what were you saying?" *Not that I care. I want to know how my Alexis is doing.*

Lisa began to ramble off again and was still talking as the love of his life and her friend walked back down the hall towards him, an exhausted look upon her beautiful face. This time Scott made sure to make eye contact with both women.

Barely slowing, both of the approaching women gave him the proper greeting due him because of his rank before they moved on and out of his sight. Scott noticed the medical symbol on the uniform of the woman with Alexis. *Must be a woman she works with.* Very reluctantly, he gave his attention back to the skinny blonde who stood talking *at*, not *with*, him as he counted down the minutes until he could once again leave her annoying presence.

"Was that him?" Sharon asked in a hushed voice as they climbed into the blue Subaru Impreza.

"Was that who and who is him?" Alexis returned as she fastened her seatbelt and waited for Sharon to drive off.

Waggling a long finger topped by an emerald green nail, Sharon laughed. "That handsome SEAL you were trying to avoid eye contact with."

Damn, she noticed. "I know him. Very arrogant and you know that I don't like always having to stop what I'm doing to snap out a salute or stand at attention just because they went to OCS while the rest of us 'worked' our way up."

"Um-hmm." The disbelieving sound echoed through the car.

"What was that for?" Alexis turned and looked at the woman driving them to the hospital.

"When are you going to tell him?" Green eyes met tiger eyes at the red stoplight.

Alexis's mouth worked furiously but nothing would come out. Finally, she dropped her head back against the leather headrest and groaned. "I don't know how to tell him." Sitting up, she looked at her friend who just knew way too much. "How did you know it was him?"

"Well, the angry huff you took when you saw him with that blonde, the whimper you gave as your eyes moved all over that body of his—which is sexy as hell, let me tell you. And then after we passed him, the way your hand cupped protectively around the as-of-yet nonexistent swell of your belly. Not to mention the way his eyes landed on you and didn't want to move off, almost like he was trying to commit you to memory again."

He was watching me? "I don't know what to do. Sharon, I said I was on birth control, and I was but...." Alexis ran her hand over her face.

White teeth flashed against tan skin and Sharon drove through the green light. "Must be a very, *very* potent man you have there." Rolling her eyes Alexis silently agreed. "Or it is proof positive you and he were meant to be."

Don't know about that, Sharon. "Hmm."

"Girl, if I had a man like that looking at me like he looked at you...damn. I wouldn't be single, that's for sure."

Arching an eyebrow, Alexis said. "Sharon, you *aren't* single. You're married."

Sharon turned into the parking lot. "Oh, yeah. Hmm. Well, don't tell the hub I forgot, okay?" she replied with a wink as they got out of the car and walked into the hospital.

※

The peach dress fit Alexis beautifully. It stopped just below her knees and formed to her body, leaving nothing to the imagination. She had matching heels on her feet that brought her a little closer to the height of the man with her, but not all the way. Thick, wavy hair had been left free to fall around her shoulders.

The man was dressed in a very nice dark gray suit. It was made to fit his broad, muscular physique and accentuated all of his fluid motions. As they walked to the table, his hand was settled comfortably on the small of her back. They made a striking couple.

"I'm pregnant." Alexis blurted out after they had been left alone by the waiter. She stared across the table at the man and waited for his response. Nervous fingers beat out a staccato rhythm on the linen tablecloth. *Please don't be mad. Don't be angry or disappointed.*

"How in the hell did this happen?" he growled in a low voice, his thick hands clenching into heavy fists.

Swallowing hard, Alexis took a sip of her ice water. "I think you know how it happened."

Eyes narrowed as the man tried to visibly relax. "Not what I meant. What I meant was—" He fell silent as the waiter brought them their breadsticks, not saying anything until they were by themselves once more. "Whose is it? Who the fuck is the father?!"

Chapter Twenty-Three

Well, this is going swimmingly. "Do you really need to ask that question?" Alexis's eyes glared into the ones across the table.

"Yes. Jesus, Lex. I thought you were on the Pill or something!" His hands waved around in agitation.

She slammed her hand down on the table, ignorant of the stares that fell on them at her action. "That's none of your damn business. I don't need a lecture from you!"

"What? You were expecting me to be happy? You aren't married!"

The accusation stung. Big tears welled up in her profound eyes. "Yes, I expected you to be happy. At least supportive. You aren't married, either."

The man immediately stood up and crossed around to the other side of the table, gathering her into his arms. "Alexis, honey, I'm sorry." After a kiss to her temple, he took his seat again.

With a shaky smile, her delicate hand reached across the table to lie upon his. "I know. It came as a shock to me also." *That's putting it mildly!*

The man with her placed their dinner orders before returning to their conversation. "Okay, so where does this leave us?"

"You know I love you, don't you?" she said as her eyes thanked him.

"I know. And I love you too." He grinned. "A baby. When are we due?"

"I'm ten weeks or about that. Can you believe it, Piers? A baby." Her voice was full of wonder.

※

A dark-haired man watched the couple eat and rise to leave. Following on their heels, he, too left the fine establishment and headed up the coast to a cabin along the beach.

Bursting through the front door, he shouted, "Scott! Scott, where the hell are you man?"

"What do you want, Reeve?" came the growling voice from beside the big bay window. "I'm busy."

Reeve Leighton walked into the living room and found his older brother sitting where he always sat, by the window looking out at the ocean. "The hell you are. I now know what is bothering you."

Blue eyes cut over to land on his brother. "What do you think you know?"

Reeve walked outside onto the deck, leaned against the railing, and allowed his response to flow back through the opened door to his brother. "Why didn't you just tell me that you and that doctor of yours broke up?"

Scott jumped up and swore as he settled along the rail beside. "What are you talking about? Who said we broke up? And for that matter, where the hell did you see her?"

Narrowing his eyes, Reeve looked out over the water. "I saw her tonight. And from what I overheard, it is not any big surprise that you have been so damn pissy lately. I mean you have been moody, but not in a long time have I seen you this jumpy."

"What are you talking about?" It was a demand for an answer, not a request.

"That she is with a man and they are pregnant." Reeve turned his head and watched his brother's reaction. The expression of anguish on his brother's face shocked him. Reeve felt bad imparting this to him, but Scott was his brother and Reeve believed he had the right to know everything.

Scott's body grew rigid. "Look, I know you weren't overly pleased meeting her, but there is no reason to lie to me like that."

"I'm not lying to you, Scott. She and this man — I can't remember his name right this second — were sitting there talking about her pregnancy and her being about ten weeks along." Reeve clapped his brother on the shoulder. "I'm sorry, man."

"What was his name?" Scott ground out between his teeth. When Reeve didn't answer right away, he shook his brother. "Damn it, Reeve! What was his name?"

"It was, it was...Pete. No, Paul, no Piers. That's it. Piers. She was with a man named Piers."

"Are you sure? Reeve, think very carefully and make sure you are positive that was the name she called him."

Reeve nodded, glimpsing the panic and relief fighting within the blond man. "Yes, I'm sure. She called him Piers. They were very comfortable together and the affection was obvious." Brown eyes watched nervously as his brother took the news.

"Ten weeks," Scott began to pace. "Ten weeks would be about the time...the time along the cliff in San Diego area." His eyes flickered back and forth. "She would tell me, wouldn't she?"

"What are you talking about, Scott?" Reeve asked as he watched his brother warily. On one hand Scott was more animated than he had been in a long time; but on the other, he was mumbling and acting strange.

"I have to go!" Scott yelled to his brother as he ran back into the house to grab the keys to his Corvette.

"Where are you going?" Reeve hollered back.

"Piers is her brother and that baby...that baby is mine!" He was gone, leaving Reeve staring after him like he was an idiot.

In his car, Scott placed a call. Nodding as he hung up the phone, his jaw set in a grim line. "I can't believe she didn't tell me I was going to be a father!" Clenching his jaw, he shifted gears and sped off down the interstate.

As he pulled into the lot of her apartment, he slid his car into a spot and turned off the engine. He saw her vehicle there and, as he got ready to get out of his car, Scott noticed Piers leaving the building. Still, he waited.

The people who saw the muscular man get out of his car fell silent as he passed. One look at him and there wasn't a single person who wanted to confront him.

His face, chiseled and handsome, was set in a determined line. Eyes were trained on something that only he knew. The fabric of his clothing, from the dark green shirt to the black BDUs he wore, molded to his body, outlining the muscles that were so obvious even in the partial light from the lampposts surrounding the parking lot.

Each and every inch of him screamed *warrior*. His strides were sure and dogged as he approached the main door. Men stepped out of the way and women found their breath caught in their throats. It was an amazing sight to see his raw power and unwavering focus.

Single-minded purpose took him up the stairs to the third floor, immediately striding to the door that said 3B on it.

Opening the door in answer to the fierce pounding, Alexis found herself looking at the man who never seemed to be far from her thoughts. "Yes?" she queried, trying to ignore the erratic beating his presence caused in her heart.

Scott just stared at her, making Alexis feel self-conscious. Her hair was piled high on her head; she wore a cut-off sweatshirt and a pair of black shorts. He took a deep breath and his eyes dragged closed.

"What do you want?" she asked further. The sooner he stated his business, the sooner he could leave. *Not that I want him to, but it hurts to see him like this and not touch him.*

"Marry me," he blurted out.

Shocked, her eyes grew wide. "Excuse me?"

"Marry me." His eyes stared straight into hers.

If only you knew how much I want to. "What are you doing here?" Alexis asked, ignoring what he said.

Bracing his hand on the doorframe, he leaned in closer to her. "Invite me in," he purred.

What if he finds out about the baby? "You can only stay for a short time. I'm exhausted and need to get some sleep. I have a very long day tomorrow," Alexis announced as she swung the door open wider to allow him into her sanctuary.

"Why did you ignore me in Norfolk?" He waited while she shut the door before he took a seat.

Sinking down onto her couch, Alexis tucked her legs under her. "I gave you the proper respect, Commander. What do you want?"

"Marry me," he said again.

"Haven't we already discussed this?" Her voice was tired.

Scott didn't answer her. Instead, with one swift and smooth movement, he rose from his chair and plucked Alexis off the couch before striding down the hall to her room.

"What are you doing?" she asked as her body instinctively molded to his.

"Shut up, Lex. Just shut up."

Opening the door to her room, he held her with one arm as his other jerked back her satin sheets before he laid her upon them.

"Get some sleep, my healer. I will be here in the morning and we will talk then." he said, brushing a hand over her face.

"There is nothing to talk about," she slurred as her body sank gratefully into the mattress.

"Yes, there is." He was unable to stop touching her.

"No, there's not. I'm not getting married. That hasn't changed."

He brushed a tender hand over her forehead. "Sleep now."

The next morning, Alexis opened her eyes slowly. She had learned that if she did anything quickly in the morning it would send her straight into an ocean of nausea. Her eyes moved around her room and she realized she was alone.

Funny, she could have sworn Scott had been here last night. Sitting up she swung her feet over to reach the floor. *Oh, well, it was just a dream.* So thinking, she went to take a shower and start her day. Twenty minutes later, she stumbled out of her bathroom, still damp from her shower, wearing nothing but a silk bathrobe.

"When were you planning on telling me?" the voice reached her.

Why am I not surprised to find you really are here? "Telling you what?" Alexis opened her closet and pulled out a loose-fitting summer dress.

"You can't be serious?" Scott demanded as he plunked himself down on her bed as if he belonged in it with her.

Alexis met his gaze before turning and walking to her chest of drawers where she pulled out a matching set of undergarments. "Look, why don't you just tell me what you are doing here? I'm sure your blonde woman is missing you."

Since her back was turned, she missed the predatory and arrogant grin that crossed his face. "She doesn't mean a damn thing to me," he purred.

Alexis jumped because his voice was now right in her ear. "Whatever." She tried to sound nonchalant.

Strong arms placed themselves on either side of her, effectively trapping her against the dresser. "We will deal with that later. When were you going to tell me we were having a baby?"

Her head dropped against the smooth wood. Alexis knew it was pointless to try and deny it. There was pooch of her belly now. "How did you find out?"

"Later." Scott spun her around so they were eye to eye. "When were you going to tell me?"

"I don't know," she admitted truthfully. "At least now I know why you said 'marry me.'"

Those bedroom eyes of his narrowed. "Don't start, Alexis. I am furious enough over the fact you didn't think I had a right to know I am going to be a father."

"I just found out myself a little while ago. And why are you so damn sure it's yours?"

He arched a blond eyebrow at that. "Because I know you, Alexis. You aren't the kind of woman who sleeps around. Don't try to pick a fight because I'm not biting."

"What if I want to fight?" She shoved against his chest suddenly. Unprepared for the assault, Scott stumbled back and watched as hysteria filled her normally serene and composed features. "What if I want to hit you? Scream at you?" Her voice rose to a shrill pitch.

"Then go ahead. Alexis, you can hit, scream, yell, whatever. I'm not going anywhere. No more games, no more of letting you whine and push me away." Scott closed the distance between them again.

Alexis backed up, her chest heaving. The tears had begun to pool in her captivating eyes. "No," she said.

"Exactly. No. Every time you push me away it breaks my heart, even more so because I know you love me. Lex, we're about to have a baby together. And you know I love you."

"I don't know anything except that I am pregnant. Single and pregnant." Her legs gave out and she would have slid to the ground if not for the quick reflexes of the man before her.

"And I am right here, offering to marry you."

"That's the problem. You feel like you need to offer it. I don't want to be in a marriage just for the child."

"If you weren't carrying my child, I would shake you for that stupid-assed comment," he hissed as he set her carefully on her feet. "I have wanted to marry you since long before this and you know it. Why are you doing this?" His fingers dug gently into her chin, forcing her to look at him. "Why can't you let me take care of you?"

Why can't you let me take care of you? That phrase echoed through her mind as she tried to back away from him. Her mind grew fuzzy and spots began to swim before her eyes. Alexis could see that firm mouth of Scott's moving but she couldn't hear anything.

Chapter Twenty-Four

Fear unlike any Scott had ever known flooded his body as he watched Alexis's eyes roll into the back of her head and her body crumple, seemingly boneless, towards the floor.

His body went into automatic mode and he barely managed to catch her before she collapsed on the hardwood floor of her bedroom. Grabbing her purse, he carried her, clad in nothing but her robe, down to his vehicle and drove them to the hospital.

Parking in the emergency zone, he carried her inside the hospital and yelled for help. As orderlies placed Alexis on a gurney and a resident checked her in, he moved his car to an appropriate parking spot before going back to stay with her. The longer it took her to regain consciousness, the more concerned and frightened he became.

It wasn't possible for Scott to live without Alexis in his life. That fact grew more and more apparent every time their paths crossed. This final stint of her collapse only sealed it. They were going to be a couple and they were going to be together.

A few hours later, Alexis opened her eyes slowly. Blinking, she found herself looking into a very familiar pair of blue eyes. "What happened? How did I get here?"

His face was full of concern as he touched her cheek. "How do you feel? Jesus, Lex, you scared me. You just collapsed! I'll get the nurse; just one sec." He moved away from her only to return moments later with a nurse.

"How are you feeling?" the nurse asked as she checked the monitors hooked up to Alexis.

"Fine. Can I see my chart, please?" Alexis asked.

"Hon, why don't you try and relax. The doctor will be here soon. He can explain things to you."

"Lady, give me my chart. I'm a doctor, I can read them," Alexis snapped.

Perhaps a bit surprised, the nurse nodded and handed over the chart before she left the curtained area. Alexis didn't even look up at the departure, too busy reading the notes.

As she did all of this, Scott watched her, his own heartbeat finally returning to normal. Moving close to the bed, Scott reached out and ran two knuckles down her cheek, drawing her eyes toward his face. "What does it say?" he asked, sitting down on the edge of the bed, He was reluctant to stop touching her for fear of losing her.

"It says," a deep voice reached them, breaking the look between them, "that she is very lucky you were around."

"Gunner!" Alexis exclaimed softly, holding out her hand towards him. "Oh, my God, it is so good to see you! I'd get up but..." She shrugged.

The doctor walked over to the free side of the bed and kissed her cheek. "Don't get up. Lord, Lexi, it is so good to see you." His hand captured hers and squeezed.

Scott's blue eyes narrowed dangerously. They were uncertain as they took in the doctor, a tall man, with dark brown hair that was in a close, neat cut. His eyes were startlingly gray. His skin was tanned and, while Scott knew he was broader, the man wearing the white coat was no slouch.

"How are you doing, Gunner?" Alexis asked, not even trying to get him to drop her hand.

"We will talk about me in a minute. What the hell is going on with you? What brought this on?" His dark eyebrows rose as he speared her with a glance.

"I was just overly exhausted. I had been doing the whole eighteen-hour, thirty-six-hour thing. You know how it is." She shrugged once more. "I'm better now. I want to go home."

"Of course you do. I am waiting on another test to make sure the baby is okay. Then you can go. But not alone." Gray eyes cut over to finally acknowledge Scott. "Will you be with her?"

"I will stay with her even if I have to kidnap her and put her somewhere she can't escape." Intense blue eyes held Alexis's.

"Good," the doctor said. "I'm Dr. Giambi, by the way. Gunner is just fine." The two men shook hands.

"Where do you know *my* Alexis from?" Scott asked.

Gunner grinned. "I've known Lexi since medical school. From your attitude, I am going to assume you are the father?"

"Yes."

Gunner smiled. "Well, in that case, congratulations…" He waited for the name to be supplied.

"Scott. Lieutenant Commander Scott Leighton," the SEAL filled in, more than a bit arrogantly.

Gunner began to laugh. "Calm down, man, don't worry. I love this little lady but I love my wife more."

Scott visibly relaxed and turned his gaze away from the chuckling doctor to Alexis. She'd fallen back to sleep. Her thick lashes rested peacefully against smooth cheeks. "I want to take her home. Is our baby okay?" he asked, watching another nurse hand the doctor a clipboard.

Looking over the sheet, Gunner nodded. "Everything is fine with your baby. I will write up some instructions for Lexi to follow. She needs to take it easy for a couple of days. I will say this once." His gray eyes grew serious. "The baby will not be fine if she continues to work herself to the ground *and* keep that much stress bottled up."

Gunner began to write some things down. "She can work hard, that's fine, because she is strong. But all that stress and lack of good sleep will only make it harder for her body to accept and healthily maintain the life she is carrying." Ripping off the paper, he handed it to Scott. "And that is the most important thing."

I couldn't agree more. "Tell me what I have to do." So while Alexis slept between them, Gunner filled in a wide-eyed Scott on the care and feeding of a pregnant woman. The military man's often hands strayed to touch the sleeping beauty between them.

※

Alexis was so comfortable. Her exhausted body stayed snuggled into the thick mattress. It felt so good as it cradled her. But no matter how wonderful it felt, she knew it wasn't her bed.

Her eyes opened and she didn't even recognize the room. Sitting up, she noticed she was totally naked between the platinum silver silk sheets. Keeping the cool material tucked around her chest, Alexis slid out of the large bed and stopped as her feet sank into the sinfully plush pale gold carpet.

"Where the hell am I?" she asked the empty room. "And where the hell are my clothes?" She pulled open all the drawers in the room and looked in the closet, not finding anything to wear. "What the hell? I can't find a damn thing to put on."

"And you won't find any." The masculine voice stunned her.

Spinning toward the voice, her thick wavy hair floated out before settling gently around her shoulders. "Scott," she breathed as her hands tightened on the sheet.

"Morning, my sexy mother-to-be." He crossed the room looking suave in his khakis and black shirt.

Holding up her hand before he could kiss her she spoke. "Where am I?"

"Give me a kiss first."

"I have to go to work today. Where are my clothes?"

"Kiss me," he murmured as his long fingers slid sensually over the silk barely covering her body.

Unable to resist, Alexis moved easily into his embrace. Her arms wrapped around his neck as their lips met. It was a gentle, exploring kiss that rapidly morphed into a heated exchange.

The sheet fell forgotten to the floor as calloused hands moved over the body of the naked woman. "I love you, Lex, please believe me," he whispered as his hands pulled her tighter against his own body.

Her hair tickled the small of her back as she allowed her head to drop back from the exquisite feel of having his hands on her body again. "I'm scared to," she responded in the same quiet voice and her head slowly moved up so their eyes could meet.

"What are you scared of?" he asked.

"Being hurt." Her hands moved over corded forearms, following their movement with her eyes.

"Look at me, Alexis," came his order. Slowly, her eyes rose up to meet his. "I will never hurt you. I could never hurt you."

"We are too different."

"Excuses, Alexis. We are going to be parents. I want to do that as a family." His mouth settled back over hers, stroking her embers into flames.

She tugged on his shirt, her message clear. "Love me, Scott, just love me." Her words flowed past his lips to settle into his soul.

"For as long as there is a breath in my body I will do just that." His clothes were gone in seconds as he laid her back on the bed and settled himself between her legs. He said with a half smile, "Guess I don't need to worry about protection anymore, do I?"

Alexis narrowed her eyes but before she could form a word in response he slid fully into her welcoming heat. "*Ohhhh,*" was all she could say.

"Tell me you love me," he begged as his body moved within hers.

"I love you. I love you, Scott." Her hips rose, drawing him in deeper as dark fingers gripped the silken material beneath her.

"Again," he commanded, as he moved faster.

"I love you!" she yelled to the room and her body exploded into a million tiny little pieces.

Scott drove deep within her one more time and he came intensely into her womb, coating it with his sperm as he, too, shouted to the room. He fell forward, stopping only because his strong arms halted him millimeters away from crushing her.

"Is this how you do pushups?" she asked, kissing him lightly.

His mouth returned the favor. "I would do a million of them if you were beneath me."

"I can barely do three," she said.

"I'll help you. Besides, you said you wanted to learn how to defend yourself." His tongue traced along the swell of her neck.

Her body shuddered. "That seems like a lifetime ago."

"Why did you want to learn how to defend yourself?"

"I need to be able to protect myself," Alexis retorted, hitting his arms in the joint so he pressed against her fully.

"Against what?" he growled. "And don't do that. I could have hurt you or Junior."

Her eyebrows rose. "Junior?"

"Well, I can't call my baby an 'it', now can I?" He rolled off her and drew her into his embrace.

"I really have to go," she said even while her body accepted his silent strength.

"No, you are on a three-day leave. Doctor's orders," he answered as his chin settled upon the top of her head.

"Well, in that case," she muttered in a coy voice. "I'm sure there is something that you promised me, like a full-body massage." Her shoulder nudged him in the chest as he grunted almost disbelievingly. "Come on, now. Don't want the mother of your child getting tense, now, do you?"

"Full body massage?" He untangled their bodies and rolled her over so she was lying on her belly. "Don't move. I will be right back."

Head turned towards the left, Alexis noticed the room fell darker as he drew the shades and turned on some low, smooth jazz. The bed dipped as his large body settled back on the mattress with her.

Large hands touched her shoulders and she felt the smoothness of the oil he had on them. The room began to smell like sandalwood and eucalyptus. His movements were just strong enough to be effective but not so hard they would be painful.

Deliberate motions went all over her back, down the back of her arms, her neck. They spread across her firm buttocks and down the backs of her legs and onto her feet. A quivering mass of Jell-o, Alexis had no resistance when he repositioned her on her back.

Scott poured more oil over her now slightly rounded body. He hadn't said a single word since the massage began and still remained silent. The only parts of him talking were his eyes and his hands. Nothing verbal.

Alexis closed her eyes and just felt his touch when he began once again with her feet, this time rubbing the tops of them. His strong fingers sent her body to a whole new plane of pleasure.

His hands worked their magic as they moved up one leg and then the other. It was amazing how good the gently sliding, massive hands felt on her body. The massage was not sexual, at least not for Alexis. She was just learning to relax and the man who wielded those miraculous hands was doing a damn good job.

Up her belly, over her increasingly tender breasts, and down each arm he rubbed, kneaded, and delivered satisfaction. By the time his hands reached her face, Alexis was sound asleep, so she missed it when, ever so gently, Scott kissed her eyelids and gathered her oiled form against his hard, naked body before he covered them with the sheet he had picked up previously.

"I'm your daddy. I will always love you and your momma." The whispered voice and the light touch on her abdomen helped to awaken Alexis from the most sated sleep she'd had in months. Extremely relaxed, Alexis didn't move right away; she just lay on her back and listened to the masculine voice that was so exceptionally tender.

"I don't care whether you are a boy or a girl. I am going to love you so much. In fact, I already do. I can't wait to meet you." More feathery touches on her stomach.

Scott's voice continued. "You are in the safest place for you right now. Your momma loves you and will keep you safe. I will keep your momma safe and when you arrive, we will both keep you safe."

"Of course, your mother is stubborn. Like right now she's eavesdropping on us instead of sleeping like the doctor ordered." Alexis's body jerked slightly. In a louder voice, he spoke to her, "I knew the second you awoke, my sexy healer. You need to sleep."

Alexis touched the back of his head and smiled as she realized just how close to her abdomen he had his face. "I'm hungry."

"There you have it, my little sailor." His voice was once again low. "Your mother is hungry. That is where I come in. As your father, it is my job to provide for your mother and you. Perhaps while I am getting her some food, you can put in a good word for me and help me convince her to marry me."

Tears welled up in her eyes as she felt his lips press against her belly. "I will always love you, my little sailor." Alexis almost missed the hushed whisper. She was still trying to blink the tears away when a blond head moved up beside her. Scott kissed her gently and sighed against her mouth, "I will always love you as well, my sexy healer."

His large body curled around hers and strong hands covered her softer ones as they settled on her belly. "What did you want to eat?" he asked softly, his eyes closed as if he just enjoyed holding her.

Alexis pulled one hand out from under his and began to move it up and down along the light blond fur on his arm. "I am going to want a military wedding, formal dress, swords…you know, the whole nine yards."

Scott eyes flew open. "What did you say?"

"I think you heard me," she said quietly.

"I heard you, but I need to hear it again," he muttered in her ear.

His heart was beating hard at her back. "I said I want the whole nine yards."

"Are you marrying me because of the baby or because you love me?"

"Both." At the tensing of his warrior's body, she added. "But the baby wouldn't be here if I didn't love you." Alexis rolled over in his arms so they were nose to nose. "I love you, Commander Leighton, and I would be proud to be your wife. If the offer is still open…"

Blue eyes filled with so much love it spilled over. "That was one offer that was never going to close. I will never let you go, Alexis Milele. You do know that, don't you? This is binding for eternity."

"Don't make promises you can't keep, Commander," she purred, running one finger down his stubble-covered jaw line.

"I don't. We belong together. I have known that since the first time I laid eyes on you. It was a feeling that grew stronger and stronger every time I saw you. I don't want to live without you. But let me ask again."

Scott placed his powerful hands on either side of her face, his eyes sincere as they caught and held her gaze. "Alexis Milele Rogets, will you marry me?"

Chapter Twenty-Five

"Oh, my God!" The screech filled the hospital break room. "Of course I will! I can't believe it. Finally!" Sharon shrieked and hugged her friend.

"Thank you, Sharon," Alexis said sitting down at the table. "It is going to be formal for the men, but I have dresses in mind for my bridesmaids."

The blonde took a seat beside her and whispered conspiratorially, "I can't believe he really proposed in bed. Damn, girl, I would love to go to bed with that!" She smiled. "Sorry, but you have got to admit he is one fine-assed man!"

"I know, believe me. I know." Alexis winked. "I have to contact a few more women and make sure they can come as well. It is going to be in September."

"That soon? How many will there be, total?"

"Seven." At her wide-eyed look, Alexis said, "Scott wanted his whole SEAL team to stand up with him."

"Are all of them officers?"

"Nope. Why?"

"No reason. Are any of them single?" Sharon grinned.

"All but one, well two, if you include the groom-to-be." Alexis shook her head at her friend. It was as if the woman had forgotten she was happily married.

"I am so happy for you! I haven't seen you look this content since you got here." Sharon touched her shoulder gently. "He's a good man for you, Lex."

"Thank you," a masculine voice interrupted. Both women turned to see Scott striding towards them, looking mouthwateringly delectable as usual. He leaned down for a kiss from Alexis and smiled at Sharon. "I think I'm a good man for her too. Scott Leighton." He offered his hand.

"Sharon Beacher. Nice to meet you, sir."

"Call me Scott, please. I'm not in uniform." His intense blue eyes fell back to Alexis and he asked her, "What time will you be home?"

"I am going to my home about eight. Why?"

"So I can have dinner ready. And I was going to be there waiting for you. I came for your key." He held his hand out expectantly.

"Pushy man," Alexis snapped as she rose to get her key from the locker.

"You like it when I push," he quipped, following her to the gray locker and waiting patiently for her to hand him the key. He grasped it and her hand. "See you at home, my sexy healer." After a lengthy kiss for Alexis, he caressed her belly and muttered, "You, as well, my little sailor." Then he was gone, leaving with that same fluidity with which he had arrived.

Alexis turned to see Sharon fanning herself. "Damn, Lex, I'm jealous. That is one man that makes my bones melt!"

"Don't let your husband hear you say that. But you are right, he does have that affect on me as well." Fanning her flushed face also, Alexis left the break room with her friend and went back to work.

※

"Mom, Dad, this is Alexis. My fiancée. We are getting married the last Saturday in September," Scott announced as he stood beside the quiet woman in the atrium of his parents' mansion.

Silence reigned while the older couple fought to keep the shocked expressions off their faces. "Harrington Prescott Broderick Leighton, what the hell is the meaning of this?!" his mother hissed.

"The meaning, Mother, is that we are getting married and are inviting you to the wedding. The invitations aren't done yet and we wanted to tell you in person." He held up one hand as his mother opened her mouth. "It is not a matter up for discussion, Mother. I love her. I'm going to marry her. End of story."

"Say something to your son!" the narrow-faced woman ordered her husband.

With a deep breath, Scott's father swallowed and said softly, "Congratulations, son." Turning his blue eyes on the woman standing with him, he added, "Nice to meet you, Alexis."

"That's it?!" Mrs. Leighton screamed. "That is all you are going to say to him for marrying that...that...that—"

"Mother," the deadly calm voice filled the area. "I would advise you to not even begin to finish that sentence." Scott shook his head, his disappointed gaze alternating between his parents. "I am ashamed that I brought her here, that you are still stuck in that stupid mindset. Father, I hope you will be there. Mother...goodbye."

Turning around with Alexis in his protective embrace, he walked out the door. "I'm so sorry, Lex. I had hoped that my family would be better." His lips brushed her temple as he helped her into his car.

"Hey, it's not your fault. You can't control how your parents feel." Alexis tried to keep her voice as light as possible and Scott knew it.

Gently turning her face towards his, he peered into her eyes. "I choose you over my family. You are my family now, you and *our* baby. My parents and I have never entirely seen eye to eye on the whole race issue, but I was hoping they would still be happy for me. I am not letting them run my life. You are my life, Lex. I love you."

"I love you, too, Scott." Leaning forward, she brushed her lips over his.

Moaning with frustration, he pulled away. "Are you sure you have to go meet Sharon?"

"Yes, I need to get the dress. It's not like I am getting skinnier before the big day. I feel like I am gaining five pounds a day," Alexis complained.

Starting the car, he laughed. "Sweetie, you have barely gained anything. Your breasts are getting bigger and the swell of your belly, but not much." Capturing her hand, he kissed the back of it. "You will be the most beautiful bride the Navy has ever had."

She climbed out of the car as he stopped in front of a bridal shop. "I will meet you at the restaurant no later than seven. We have reservations for seven-fifteen." Waving over her shoulder at him she disappeared into the store where Sharon was waiting for her.

At seven-fifteen exactly, Alexis walked beside her handsome fiancée through the restaurant. The engagement ring he had picked up that day shone on her slim finger. The solitaire diamond was two and a half carats in a brilliant cut, set in a gold band. She wore an elegant floral dress and Scott was in a dark blue suit.

Her body relaxed a bit as Scott's increasingly familiar touch caressed her between her shoulder blades. "Relax, my love," his voice caressed her.

"I'm nervous," she admitted looking at him.

"You've already met Reeve. It will be okay. I'll make it up to you later, I promise," he crooned.

This afternoon with your parents didn't go okay. "I'm not feeling so hot," she mumbled as her hand rested protectively on her belly.

"Lex," he said, halting their movement.

She looked up to meet his smoldering gaze. "What?"

"Just this." Scott's lips found hers and he kissed her until her body sagged against him.

"Okay," she slurred, licking her lips to further prolong the taste that was purely Scott.

"Ready now?"

"Keep kissing me like that and I will be ready for anything." She ran her hand lightly over his firm ass.

"Let's do this, then. They're right over there." He pointed to their destination.

Alexis watched the two men at the table stand as they approached. "Evening, Alexis," Reeve said with a smile and pressed a quick kiss to her cheek before slapping his brother on the shoulder.

Scott nodded and smiled. "Evening, Godric." He shook his youngest brother's hand and leaned down to kiss his sister. "Corliss. I want both of you to meet Alexis. Alexis, the rest of my family. Godric and Corliss."

"Nice to meet you both," Alexis said, smiling gently.

"A pleasure," Godric said, shaking her hand.

"Nice to meet you," Corliss responded with a smile of her own.

"Scott tells me you are in medical school," Alexis said to Corliss, feeling a bit more comfortable talking about that, familiar ground for both of them.

By the end of the evening Alexis felt fine with the two younger siblings. They had warmed up considerably during dinner. Both were attending the wedding and were exuberant about their upcoming niece or nephew. Even so, as Scott drove them away from the restaurant, she was exhausted.

Emotions were still running high and they still had to deal with her side of the family. Allowing the cool night air to pour over her face, Alexis closed her eyes and just enjoyed the touch of Scott's hand on her thigh.

"Feeling okay over there?" he asked over the wind.

She squeezed his hand. "Fine. Just thinking."

"They loved you. And I know that Corliss is thrilled to have a doctor in the family so she can have someone to talk to about the trials of med school." Slanting a sideways glance at her, his brows converged slightly, as he noticed the strain on her face. "What's wrong, Alexis?"

Head lolling on the headrest, she opened her eyes to look at the man driving the Corvette. "This is happening so fast. I am just getting overwhelmed."

"Second thoughts?" He pulled into the driveway of his cabin and turned off the car.

"Yes," she answered honestly.

"Let's take a walk." Helping her out of the car, he led her down to the beach and they strolled along the sand as the moon shone down upon them. "Second thoughts about marrying me? Having my baby? What?"

"Second thoughts about getting married so fast." Alexis slid her arm around his waist as his arm settled around her shoulder. "Not about marrying you and never about the baby. Just that I don't want it to be a rushed thing and that is what it's feeling like. It is less than a month away. I haven't even told my parents."

Stopping her, he touched her forehead with his own. "Everything is set on my end. What can I do to help you?"

"I don't know," she complained as her hands bunched the jacket of his suit.

"How about I take care of the food and music? I will even go talk to the chaplain and get that set."

"Really? You'd do that for me?"

"No, I'd do it for us." He kissed her. "And I am going to start looking for a house."

She drew back. "Why?"

"Well, we aren't living in two different places. I'm not that easy-going."

"What's wrong with your cabin?"

"You'd live here?"

"Are you serious? I love your cabin. And have since the first time I saw it." Stepping closer, Alexis placed her head on his chest, sighing contentedly as his heartbeat soothed her nerves.

"We will live there, then. I will work on getting your things moved in." Strong arms wrapped around her, cocooning her in his Herculean strength.

"Okay," she whispered as nature flowed over her. The sounds of the ocean, his steady heartbeat, and the wind soothed her.

"I love you, Lex," he whispered.

"Love you, too, Commander."

※

"You what?! What?!" The shriek was amazingly loud considering how far it had to travel. It sounded like Alexis's mother was in the room with her instead of up the coast in Maine.

"I'm getting married, Mother. The end of September. That last Saturday, and you and Dad are invited. The invitations are on the way but I wanted to call you before hand."

"Who is he?" Her father's calm voice reached her. Her parents were on speakerphone.

"He is a lieutenant commander in the Navy. And a SEAL." She held the phone away from her ear as her mother began to scream again. When she finished, Alexis brought it back and continued. "Before you ask, no, he isn't a brother. He's white."

"Does he make you happy, Lex?" her father asked.

"More than I ever believed possible, Daddy." Alexis smiled as the man she was talking about walked by with his brother as they made plans for the wedding. Godric had offered his country club for the location and planned on supplying the food.

"In that case, congratulations," her father said.

"Are you pregnant?" Her mother sounded accusatory.

"Yes, ma'am, I am," Alexis confirmed softly.

"I see," her mother said. "Well, you know him, I don't."

"I love him, Mother. And he loves me and this baby. Please be here with me on this day," Alexis implored.

"Baby, I may not always agree with your choices or how you go about doing things, but I am always going to support you. We will be there. Is there anything I can do on this end?" Her mother's tone had softened considerably.

"See if you can get in touch with Gamaliel. I would love him to be there."

"Did you want him to preside?" Mrs. Rogets questioned.

"No, ma'am. It's a military wedding. The chaplain will do it." Alexis smiled when Scott winked at her.

"Very well, then. We will get in touch with him and be there a few days before the wedding. Love you, little girl," her father said.

"Bye, Daddy. Love you too. Bye, Mother." Alexis disconnected the call and groaned as she put the phone back in the charger.

"Everything go okay?" Scott asked, poking his head in the room.

"Peachy. I am just taking a break before I call the other brothers. Mom said she was going to try and get a hold of Gamaliel."

"Godric and I are going to go run some errands. Will you be okay?" he asked as he walked over to her and kissed her.

She stroked his face. "Yes. *We'll* be fine. After I make these calls I have to get to work. I have the late shift today."

"Okay. I'll see you later. Love me?"

"Love you."

"Good." He kissed her again and was gone.

Alexis showered and got ready for work before she called the three brothers she could get in contact with: Piers first, since he already knew she was pregnant, then she called Maurice, and finally had to leave a message with Kieran's secretary since he was working out of the office.

As Alexis climbed into her Expedition, she smiled and took a deep breath. Life was good. She was getting married, having a baby, and it didn't hurt that those things were happening with the same guy. In two and a half weeks and she would be Mrs. Leighton. Wow.

A huge smile was on her face as she got to work, but it faded when she got a call. Sharon was with her as she tried to control her breathing at the news Scott and his team had just been deployed to "resolve" a situation.

I'm still getting married, right? He would make it back, wouldn't he? Swallowing back the bile, Alexis worked and tried not to think about it.

Chapter Twenty-Six

Alexis was scared, exhilarated, and nauseous.

The big day had finally arrived, and the men had returned home safely from their mission in time for the rehearsal. Never before had the sight of eight men ever looked so good to her. As Scott when had closed his arms around her, she'd felt like her world was once again safe and orderly. To the cheers of one and all, she and her SEAL had kissed until both of them were weak-kneed.

Her family and friends had had to drag them apart. Neither had wanted to be separated that night, but tradition was tradition. So now here she stood in the large cathedral, hidden from the view of her husband-to-be.

"You are beautiful, Lex," her father said as he appeared behind her.

"Thank you, Daddy." Alexis smiled as her eyes looked at him in the reflection of the vanity mirror. He made a handsome figure in his tuxedo. "You look amazing."

As Katie, her maid-of-honor, set the headpiece on her head and lowered the veil, every eye in the room began to tear up. "Goodbye, Ms. Rogets," Alexis heard her whisper.

"Are you ready?" her father asked as one by one the bridesmaids left to walk up the aisle.

"I think so. I'm so freaking nervous, I think I will trip!"

"You will be fine, baby. He's a good man for you, honey. He'll make you happy."

"He already does, Daddy. He already does." They were in front of the doors waiting for the music to cue them in. The coordinator gave a last-minute fix to the train and the bottom of her dress. The wedding march began and two ushers soundlessly swung open the double doors leading to the main part of the church.

Through the many layers of her veil, Alexis saw her future waiting for her at the end of the aisle. The bridesmaids wore the same style dress but in different colors that flattered individual wearer. All seven women were a beautiful sight.

The right side of the church was white. Every man up there wore white military formal dress uniforms. All black shoes were spotless and each officer's sword, she knew, would gleam in the sun once they were drawn. At the head of them stood her future husband. The love of her life.

Ramrod straight, uniform perfectly creased, ribbons and medals on his chest, Scott carved an impressive figure. Even beneath the veil, Alexis felt herself blush as his gaze moved up and down her body as if he could see under her dress. One corner of his mouth turned up and he nodded as if responding to something that was whispered to him.

Scott was frozen to the spot as he watched Alexis come through the doors on her father's arm. She was radiant. He had never before seen someone so beautiful.

The dress hid the fact she was pregnant. Not that he minded, but he knew she'd been concerned about it. The sweetheart neckline only enhanced her full bosom. Long, lacy sleeves converged to a point on the back of her smooth, dark hands. A full skirt of satin trimmed with lace flowed around her as she walked.

Each step brought her closer to him. To their life together. The veil hid her face from view and he spied the long train that followed behind her. She clasped a beautiful bouquet of white roses in her hands as she came closer and closer.

His eyes moved up and down her body until he heard Tyson, his best man say, "Breathe, man." Greedily, Scott took air in and his mouth fluttered into a one-sided grin as he realized just how close he'd been to passing out.

It would never stop amazing him, this woman of his, this woman who could bring him to his knees with nothing more than a smile. Swallowing to control the rampaging emotions that were pounding though his belly like a herd of hippopotami, Scott put his cornflower-blue gaze on the love of his life, the mother of his unborn child, and felt the tears begin to form.

Both Scott and Alexis were in a daze when the ceremony ended. As tan fingers lifted the veil layers for their first kiss as a wedded couple, Scott's strong hands trembled. Their lips, however, met without any hesitation and the rest of the room faded into nothing.

For a while the new couple stood locked in an embrace that showed everyone there just how much they loved each other. It took a while before the cheering broke into their world.

"I love you, Alexis Leighton," he said as his teary gaze met hers.

"And I you, Commander, and I you." Her manicured fingers wiped away the tears from the corner of his eyes.

Pausing at the top of the cathedral steps, the chaplain announced, "For the first time in public, it gives me great pleasure to present Lieutenant Commander and Mrs. Leighton." The crowd outside erupted in cheers.

Standing beside her husband, Alexis looked down the five steps and saw sixteen naval officers lining the walk to the limo, eight on each side. Closest to the car was Tyson and he gave the orders for the men to "present arms." His deep voice filled the air. "Draw," pause, "Swords." Once that was done, he commanded, "Blades to the wind."

Arm in arm, Scott and Alexis walked under the canopy of swords. As they passed Tyson and Maverick, who were the last two, a sword smacked her across the rump as "Go Navy!" was bellowed. After they were through, Tyson ordered, "Return swords. Dismissed."

Then it was into the limo and on to the reception at the country club.

"I have been waiting to do this for a long time now," Tag said as he approached the happy couple. "I am going to kiss the bride."

Alexis grinned at the pilot as he fixed his uniform before strutting closer to her. "Keep in mind whose woman she is, Tag, if you plan on flying ever again," came Scott's warning.

"I'm allowed to kiss the bride. It's tradition," the handsome pilot gloated.

"So is the husband's jealousy," Scott growled.

Tag walked up to Alexis and planted a big kiss on her, tipping her backwards and everything. Just before Scott ripped him away from her, he stood her up and stepped back. "Wow," he said licking his lips. "That was some kiss."

Alexis just stood there blinking. Scott noticed and sighed. He couldn't even really be angry at them.

A touch on his arm and he looked down at his lovely bride. "What is it, sweetheart?"

"Look who just arrived." She pointed to the door where Scott saw his father and mother walk in, dressed to the nines. He was relieved to see them. Alexis's family had been wonderful, accepting him upon sight, but he'd felt a bit sad not to see his own parents at the ceremony.

"Go talk to them," Alexis urged. "I'm going to go dance."

With a kiss to Alexis's forehead, he went to do just that.

That night, as the moon shone down on the ocean, two lovers walked hand-in-hand along the deserted beach. Waves lapped at their feet as the man finally stopped and gathered the woman into his arms.

"I love you, healer of my heart," the man murmured softly.

Dropping her head back so she could meet his eyes in the muted light, the woman responded, "And I love you, my husband."

Scott brushed his lips against hers. "I will never get tired of hearing you call me that."

"Thank you. For not giving up on me." Alexis smiled. "For not giving up on us."

"Oh, Lex, how could I give up on us when we were meant to be? Our destiny was written in the stars."

Turning in his embrace so she could stare out over her beloved ocean, Alexis inhaled deeply. A gentle smile crossed her face as she imagined what their life together would bring.

Without a word, the Navy SEAL swept his wife up in his arms. Even pregnant, she hardly weighed anything to him. He carried her back up the beach, leaving behind the outside world for the chance to be with the woman who made him a better man. The woman who had healed him.

The twinkling stars and the waning moon filtered down light on the couple as they began their new life together. There were no interruptions from beepers or phones, just two people whose lives had become irrevocably intertwined. They made love until the moon set beyond the horizon and the sun began to climb in the sky.

Clear of clouds, it was an omen of good things to come. On the chaise on the porch, the warm sun fell upon a couple covered by a blanket. The man had his body curled protectively around the woman and his hand cupped her belly as if guarding the life that grew in there as well.

The woman was asleep but the man was awake, gazing at her and their unborn baby. "I love you, Alexis Milele Leighton."

As the sun watched over him, he watched over his family. As his wife slept, Scott, too, began to give in to the lure of the sandman. Almost reluctant to close his eyes for fear it might all be a dream, his hold on her body tightened as he finally drifted off to sleep.

A Navy SEAL nicknamed Harrier and Alexis, his healer, had finally found and accepted their destinies. To be together. As one. For all time.

About the Author

Aliyah Burke loves to read and write. Her debut novel, *A Knight's Vow*, was released in 2004. She loves to hear from her readers and can be reached at aliyah@aliyah-burke.com, aliyah_burke@hotmail.com, and feel free to join her yahoo group at http://groups.yahoo.com/group/aliyah_burke or friend her at http://www.myspace.com/aliyahburke. Please stop by her website, www.aliyah-burke.com for more available titles—just don't forget to sign the guestbook!

Aliyah is married to a career military man. They have a German Shepherd, a Borzoi, and a DSH cat. Her days are spent splitting her time between work, writing, and dog training.

Printed in Great Britain
by Amazon.co.uk, Ltd.,
Marston Gate.